HER OUTLAW DADDY

JANE HENRY

Copyright © 2016 by Jane Henry

Published by Stormy Night Publications and Design, LLC.
www.StormyNightPublications.com

Cover design by Korey Mae Johnson
www.koreymaejohnson.com

Images by The Killion Group and 123RF/Mykhaylo Pelin

All rights reserved.

1st Print Edition. December 2016

ISBN-13: 978-1541098183

ISBN-10: 1541098188

FOR AUDIENCES 18+ ONLY

This book is intended for adults only. Spanking and other sexual activities represented in this book are fantasies only, intended for adults.

PROLOGUE

Until we have seen someone's darkness, we don't really know who they are. Until we have forgiven someone's darkness, we don't really know what love is. — Marianne Williamson

Cole took a final drag from the stub of his smoke, tossed it down, and ground it out with the heel of his boot, watching as the remains easily blended into the soft dirt. Blowing the smoke to the side, he watched with narrowed eyes several yards ahead as the man hired as guard lazed back, his heels upon the stone wall that surrounded the Perkins estate. The guard's hat fell over his face.

"Couldn't see a hand in front of his eyes," Cole scoffed. He despised laziness. It was a damn good thing the lazy son of a bitch watchman didn't answer to Cole.

If the guard had any idea who lay waiting in the shadows of the forest, he wouldn't be lying back napping either. He'd hold that pistol that lay on the terrace by his feet with both fucking hands. More than likely, though, he'd run screaming for his life like a schoolgirl.

Cole shook his head. It'd be like taking candy from a baby. It was too bad, really. He much preferred a struggle.

Maybe he'd get lucky tonight. Maybe the girl would put

up a fight. He cracked his knuckles, a slow, wicked grin revealing white teeth against tanned skin. He'd taken a good look at her earlier, her skin as white and unblemished as newly fallen snow, her cleavage full and welcoming atop the bodice of her fitted dress. How he longed to run his dark, wicked hands through her soft blond curls and yank that hair, making her scream. Just watching her run her silver hairbrush through her long tresses as he hid in the shadow of the veranda made him hard as hell.

Her daddy would pay dearly for what he'd done.

He turned to the darkness and raised a hand, giving the signal. Four shadows moved to obey, Cole ahead of the pack. He was the one they answered to, and the largest of the crew. They'd traveled hundreds of miles to get here. And now the moment had come.

It was time to enact justice.

Judgment and damnation for all. And if things went his way, there would be pain.

CHAPTER ONE

Everyone is a moon, and has a dark side which he never shows to anybody. — Mark Twain

"Make a sound, darlin', and you'll regret it."

His voice was deep and raspy, sending a chill of fear through Aida. She gasped as she sat up in bed, instinctively scurrying backward, but with two large strides he was upon her, pinning her back down upon the bed, one hand grasping her wrists as a second whipped a bandanna from his pocket. He released her hands and tied the bandanna quickly around her mouth, the knots so tight she winced in pain. The rough fabric smelled like tobacco and bacon, and her stomach twisted. Her eyes flitted around the room, trying her best to find a means of escape. One small man stood behind her captor on the left, and a taller, thinner one on the right. She was overpowered and outnumbered, but she would not go down without a fight.

Even if she'd had warning, she never would've been able to fight off three full-grown men by herself. Swatting away flies from her lemonade on a hot summer day was about as fast and furious as her little hands had ever swung. Her eyes flew open in the darkness as her worst fears became a reality.

The blood rushed through her ears, her heart thudding, as she kicked out her foot and happily connected with her captor's stomach. He doubled over in pain, cursing, as the other two moved toward her. Swiftly, her hands momentarily freed, she grasped the glass of water on her nightstand and whipped it at the small man on her left. It hit him with a thud, water splashing all over him and the wall, as the glass fell to the floor and shattered. As the third man moved to close in on her, bending down to restrain her, she kicked her right foot out and hit him straight in the face. He howled, both hands covering his face, but the first man had already recovered. With one swift move, he pinned her wrists down on the bed, deftly tied them with the length of rope, and to her shock, twisted her over on her side, smacking his palm against her thinly clad backside. Half a dozen vicious, searing swats took her breath away and made tears come to her eyes. She cried out, but couldn't escape, the bandanna gagging her screams, the rope making her helpless to fight him.

His arms came around her, lifting her straight off the bed and over his shoulder as if she weighed nothing at all. Unable to defend herself with her hands, she kicked her feet as best she could, but one arm tightened around her legs as his hand came down again, blistering her backside.

Later, she would remember that he never lifted a fist to her, but only the palm of his hand on her backside.

"Y'all right?" he hissed into the darkness to the other men. But the two she'd managed to attack had recovered already and they now moved as one, following their leader to where the large window opened to the balcony, the curtains billowing in the wind. Panic rose. They were going to kidnap her. She had to get away. But even twisting with all she had, she was helpless against his grip, restrained against most movement. Shouts and the sounds of shattering glass could be heard in other parts of the house as they moved swiftly. She had two thoughts at once—first, that Lucille, her tutor and only friend, who'd been sent from them the week before, had been spared in the melee, and second, a fervent wish that someone even more savage had come for her father, and in the struggle, killed him.

• • • • • • •

As Aida woke, she kept her eyes closed. She couldn't remember at first where she was or how she'd gotten there. As her eyes remained shut tight, she lay still, trying to assess the situation as best she could. It all came back to her at once.

Beneath her back she felt warm, soft blankets, some type of Indian animal skin, perhaps. Her wrists were still bound tightly, and the rope chafed against her tender skin, along with the gag around her mouth. The chemise she'd been wearing when taken from bed felt like it was intact, though it offered her little protection. And as she lay on the ground in the dark, she could still feel the stinging on her backside, an immediate reminder of the cowboy's vicious palm the night before.

"Wakin' up, darlin'?" crooned a voice by her side, and her eyes flew open. It was her captor from the night before, the leader of the group. He still wore his bandanna over his mouth, and his eyes were trained on her. She tried to sit up, but was tied in too awkward a posture, so she struggled. He reached over, yanking her up by the shoulders so she could slouch into a seated position. He sat on the ground, knees pulled up to his chest, his arms resting lazily, but one hand reached to his waist and removed a gleaming pistol. She glared at him as he watched her, his eyes as dark as coffee, brooding and calculating.

"You sit there like a good little girl," came his low drawl as he pulled his bandanna down from his mouth. His voice was so deep and raspy it made her hair stand on end. "Now that I've gotten your attention, you'll listen to me. You listenin', darlin'? You nod that pretty little head if you're listenin'."

She glared at him.

He placed the gun on the ground and crawled over to her. Fear made the hair on her arms stand up as he reached a hand out to her, but it was only to unfasten the bandanna from her mouth. As soon as it was released, she sucked in a deep breath, pulled her face away from his hand, and spat at him, hatred boiling up inside her. She wanted to grab the bandanna around his neck and twist it around his neck. He flinched as her saliva hit his cheek, his fingers going to the back of his head and whipping off his own bandanna. He bunched up the fabric and swiped it at his face, tossing both bandannas to the ground.

He sat back, glaring. Now that his mask was removed, she was able to fully take in his appearance. His hair was dark brown, matching his coffee-colored eyes, thick stubble covering his square jaw. His features were even and rugged. If she wasn't so filled with fury at her captor, she'd consider him an attractive man, every bit a toughened cowboy or gunslinger. His jaw was clenched, his lips a thin line, as he spoke to her in his low, raspy voice.

"I know who you are," he said. "And you'll listen to me now without a fight. I'll tell you exactly what I expect of you, and you'd do well to do as I say, or I'll take that strap I have hangin' on the side of my horse, and tan your backside. You understand me, Aida Marie Perkins?"

The use of her full name and the threat of the strap made her stomach clench. She looked to the saddle of his horse, where a folded piece of sturdy leather did indeed hang, next to a stout riding quirt, ready for use. She wondered why he had it and how often he used it. He eyed her thoughtfully for a minute, his eyes filled with steely conviction. She knew in her gut he would indeed make good on his promise. Glaring at him, she nodded.

"My gripe ain't with you," he said, "but with your father. You're comin' with us as our captive, ransom against what your daddy owes us. We have a long, dangerous journey ahead of us, and there are rules you'll be expected to follow.

You hear me?"

Aida shifted, still glaring, and refused to answer. His eyes rested on the strap. Noting the silent threat, Aida felt fear claw at her chest for a quick minute. She nodded.

His eyes focused on hers for a moment before he continued. "You'll do as I say. *Everyone* in our company obeys me, you and the other four men I have with me. There's no room for disobedience or disrespect. That means you'll eat what I feed you, come when I call you, and do what I say. Anything short of complete obedience, and I'll punish you." He paused as his words sank in. "*Soundly.*" His eyes darkened. "And I'll expect you to treat me with respect. Understood?"

She glared at him, hatred a live, pulsing heat between them. Her words were a low hiss. He could whip her, he could tie her up, he could make her *obey*, but she'd let him kill her before she'd ever give him *respect*.

Though her mouth was dry, she used up what she had left as she spat again on the ground with vehemence. "You filthy scoundrel!"

He watched her through eyes so narrow they were no more than slits before he shifted up and drew even closer to her, while she cursed furiously. Though her heart thundered in her chest, she still did not regret refusing to submit. He reached a hand to where her long, wavy blond hair hung loose about her face, grabbed a fistful, and yanked so hard she felt the piercing pain along her scalp and spine. She cried out involuntarily as his mouth came to her ear.

"I gave you a choice, little girl, and I gave you one chance to do this the easy way. I'll have you know it'll be my immense pleasure to whip your gorgeous backside raw while you scream for mercy. Darlin', you just gave me exactly what I came for."

CHAPTER TWO

Stars, hide your fires; Let not light see my black and deep desires.
— *William Shakespeare*

"Up!" shouted Cole, his deep voice ringing through the early morning air. He signaled to Junior standing guard a few yards in front of where the horses were tied, and watched as the other men rose around them. Aida stumbled as he tugged her along with him, and his hands reached to her waist to steady her. It was almost a shame how easy it was to hold her. He held her by the scruff of her neck, the way an angry schoolteacher might haul a naughty child outside to be punished. With his free hand, he snagged the strap and snapped it against his leg, both to frighten her with the sound of it and to also remind him of how badly it stung. He'd used the strap to bring many men to their knees, but he'd never whipped a woman, and he was conscious of her more delicate skin and constitution. Whipping a man's toughened back wasn't the same as the lovely backside he planned to punish. Instilling fear before he whipped her would go a long way in aiding his ultimate plan. She needed to fear him. She needed to tremble in awe. She would hate him, but she would obey.

Junior turned to watch them.

"Y'all right back there, Cole?" he asked.

"Someone decided to defy me already," Cole said, dragging Aida and the strap to a wooded area. "And the sooner we get our rules straight, the better."

Junior was slight, with blue eyes and tufts of blond hair creeping out beneath the Stetson he was still growing into. His innocent looks belied his true character. The youngest recruit of Cole's, he could be tough as nails when push came to shove. Cole'd seen him pistol-whip a man twice his size in the last town they'd visited, and threaten to cut the fingers off a man who'd had the nerve to touch a lady of the line in a saloon they'd stopped at the week prior. The man hadn't asked permission, Junior had explained later, when Cole had to wrestle the knife out of Junior's hands. Junior was vicious, but his weakness was pretty ladies.

"Already?" Junior asked, frowning. "Can't you just—"

"You leave off, Junior, and don't you get in my way, unless you want a taste of the strap yourself."

Junior's eyes widened slightly. Cole had taken the strap to him once, when he was still a new recruit, only eighteen years old with much to learn. He'd gone behind Cole's back and stolen a gold pocket watch from a traveling salesman, simply because he'd liked it. Cole didn't allow defiance and didn't abide theft, unless he authorized it. Junior had taken his whipping like a man and made amends. He'd never defied Cole again. But he well knew Cole meant what he said. Holding his hands palm up, Junior backed off in surrender.

The other men didn't budge from their stations as Cole dragged Aida deeper into the woods. They all knew when Cole pronounced a sentence, it was best not to interfere. The pretty blonde within his grip screamed at him and swore as he hauled her to where a large tree served a perfect whipping post. He chuckled mirthlessly.

"Well, now, ain't you pretty puttin' up a fight. Care to repeat that last phrase, pretty girl?"

She kicked her feet and struggled against his grasp, but it was no use. He was far stronger, and enjoying every bit of the struggle.

When they got close enough to the tree, he dropped the strap to the ground. He deftly swung her around and checked her tied hands, ignoring the hatred in her eyes. He didn't care about the hatred. What he needed to see was compliance.

She'd get there.

When she was good and secured, he leaned her up against the tree, thankful she wore nothing but the thin cotton garment. There'd be no need to remove it. He knew how to swing the strap expertly so that it would fall in just the right way, delivering a satisfying burn. The strap was a softer leather than the horsewhip that lay back at the wagon, and was unlikely to welt her as easily.

"Now, pretty girl, you'll stand up against that tree and take your punishment, or I'll have to hold you over my lap. And as much as I'd like to have that lovely body of yours closer to my cock, we can get this over more quickly if you take your whippin'."

She seemed torn. Her eyes flitted to the side, as if to find an escape route, but there was none and that was exactly the way he liked it. She could either stand against the tree and be whipped, or be taken over his knee. In the end, he would get her obedience. If there was anything he could do expertly, it was extract compliance from those who were weaker.

She tossed up her chin and glared at him. "You can tie me up and whip me," she said. "But I'll see you hanged for this."

Clenching his jaw, he grabbed her about the shoulder and tried to get her into position, but her foot shot out and kicked him in the kneecap. It stung like the dickens, and he swore vehemently as he rubbed at the pain, reaching for her bound wrists, but she was too quick. She spun away and tried to run but he snagged her about the waist. She tried to pull away from him, screaming at the top of her lungs, but it was too late for her now. He ducked her swinging fist, encircled her waist with his arm, and in one swift motion, dropped to the ground, hauling her straight across one bent knee. He lifted the strap and let loose a hard, whistling lash. She screamed when the strap connected with her backside. She kicked and hollered but couldn't get away. Holding her tightly, he gave her another few measured swats with the strap. Her ferocity in fighting him still didn't wane, though her voice caught now when she screamed. With nothing to protect her from the bite of the strap but her thin cotton chemise, he plied the strap against her thighs, and heard a whimper escape. Now he was getting somewhere. He spanked her again in the same spot. She yelped, pulling away and moaning, twisting her bottom, but he knew how to overpower her so that she could do little more than kick her feet. He was bigger, stronger, and meaner.

A string of curse words flew out of her mouth. Cole's mouth set in a grim line, and he spanked her again. "Well, look what we have here," he said in a low drawl, bringing the strap down with two more vicious lashes against her upper thighs. "A pretty girl who swears like a sailor. Tsk, tsk."

Whap! The more he spanked, the more she fought. His arm hurt from having to restrain her so firmly, but he knew now wasn't the time to stop. She needed a strapping that would break her will, leaving him the decided victor. "Seems to me, little lady, that you need more than a lesson in obedience," he said, punctuating his words with whistling lashes of the strap. "Seems to me you need a lesson in manners your daddy should've taught you." *Whap! Whap!* "And since I'm the man for the job, we're not done here until you call me Daddy."

Her curses echoed through the woods. He cringed. He'd have to spank her harder. With her over his knee, his range of motion was limited, and he couldn't rear back to swing the way he would if she'd been up against the tree. Bracing himself, he lifted his hand even higher. The strap whistled through the air before landing in the hardest stroke he'd given her yet. Her whole body jerked from the sting of it, but still, she would not submit. He wouldn't use anything more severe than the strap. He wouldn't whip her harder. The point was to make her obey him, break through her stubborn resistance, not cause her real harm. He'd simply have to stay the course until she gave in.

Now he waited seconds between each lash. *Whap!* He paused, still holding her tightly, noting that now her legs didn't kick quite so hard and her voice was growing hoarse from screaming at him.

"Say, 'I'm sorry, Daddy.'"

"Go to hell!"

Whap! Another scream echoed in the woods. He waited again before he repeated his request but again, she refused. Now he waited even longer. Maybe not knowing when the next swat would fall would break her resolve. As he whipped her again, she was silent, this time only flinching as the lash landed. "I've got all day, little lady," he said. "And we're not goin' anywhere until you obey."

Again, the lash fell. She refused to submit. Still holding her under his arm, he dropped the strap. This would not do. He would have to bare her after all.

She put up another fuss as he lifted her chemise, revealing thin cotton undergarments that easily dropped open when he released the drawstring. Her bottom was as red as a ripe strawberry, the bare skin hot to the touch when he placed his large hand against her. His cock hardened beneath her as he ran his hand over her naked skin. She winced and squirmed at the intimate touch, and it took all his self-control not to touch more than he'd planned. Though seeing her restrained over his knee and resisting him made his cock bulge in his pants, now was not the time to take her.

Cole lifted his palm and brought it down on her reddened backside so hard, finger-shaped welts rose on her naked skin. He spanked her thighs, first one and then the other, curving his hand expertly so that she winced with each blow.

"Are you goin' to obey, Miss Aida?"

She shook her head, but didn't speak this time, as he administered another half a dozen swats. The sound of his hand on her bare skin rang in the stillness, but still she would not obey.

"All you have to do is say, 'I'm sorry, Daddy.'"

She shook her head again. Keeping a steady tempo, he spanked her until finally, she bent at the waist, the resistance going out of her.

"I'm sorry!" she moaned, her voice near desperate. "Please, stop! I can't take anymore!"

He delivered another crisp swat, the slap of his palm on her naked skin echoing around them. "I'm sorry, what?" he asked.

He heard a half sob escape from her mouth. He paused, and when she didn't speak, he delivered another serious swat. "What do you say, young lady?" he asked.

"I'm sorry, Daddy!"

He closed his eyes, his cock so hard it was painful, as he immediately stopped her spanking. He'd told her he'd spank her until she obeyed, and she'd obeyed. Running his large hand over her scorching hot bottom, he praised her now, though it sounded condescending even to his own ears.

"Very good. Good girl," he crooned. She was so beautiful.

She was crying freely, and he was overcome with the strong desire to hold her in his arms. But no. That would not do. He had to reinforce the lesson he'd just given her.

"Are you going to behave yourself now, or is Daddy going to have to take you over his knee again?"

She sniffled, staring at the ground. "I'll behave."

"Try that again. One more chance before I pick up the strap and start over."

"Yes, Daddy!"

He nodded, grinning wickedly. "Very good," he said. With his free hand, he righted her drawers and pulled down her chemise. He stood, still holding her elbow in his hand.

"Pick up the strap, Aida," he ordered. She frowned but obeyed as she bent and lifted the strap, handing it to him.

"Oh, no, I don't want you to hand it to me," he said. "You carry it. And when we get back to camp, you'll fix it back up near my saddle, so it's right nearby when you and I ride together later."

She hung her head and held the strap in her hand, as he took her free hand and walked her back to the wagon. She hated him, no doubt. But at least now she would obey.

CHAPTER THREE

*Love is what we were born with. Fear is what we learned here. —
Marianne Williamson*

Aida hated the jostling atop the horse, every bounce and shift causing her backside to ache. She sat in front of Cole, his arms around her as he held the reins. In any other circumstance, she might feel he was protecting her but now, she knew he sat behind her so he could watch her every move. She tried to take stock of what the men had tied to their horses, but what they carried was minimal and well-hidden, clearly so they'd be ready to gallop at a moment's notice. She noted various bundles and tins that looked like beans, cornmeal, and dried bacon, tin cups strung together for water and a handful of eating utensils. Her stomach growled, though she wouldn't admit she was hungry even if Cole whipped her again. He would not get any sign of weakness from her.

She saw the menacing strip of leather curled up and dangling from beneath his blanket, and she shuddered, squirming as her aching backside met the hard saddle. She took pride in her comely figure and delicate skin, and wondered if the brute had left any marks. No doubt he'd welted and bruised her with the whipping he'd given her. Glaring, Aida pulled her legs up closer together. Despite the cowboy's rough demeanor, she had a vague recollection of him positioning her just so on the saddle. No doubt his aim had been to keep her alive on the journey so he could deliver her to wherever they were going, and he'd had no intent on actually being *gentle*.

She looked around wildly. There had to be something, anything she could use to plan her escape. Something she could use to hurt them, and get away. All weapons were, of course, safely hidden on the men outside the wagon. Rope wasn't very useful in escaping from a band of vicious kidnappers, and she couldn't think of much else. Her eyes fixed on a few small candles tied together—again, useless. But as she continued to discreetly look at their wares, she noted the heavy iron skillet. She smiled to herself, but then frowned. What *would* her plan be? To whack the head of whomever she was closest to? Then what? Smack the other men? She sighed. She'd no doubt end up tied up and whipped again.

Her heart stuttered as the horse drew to a halt. She sat up, smoothing a hand over her chemise and hair. Though she was surrounded by a band of savage, wild men, it was still habit to fix herself and look as presentable as possible, something she'd been taught since before she could even walk. She hoped they'd actually give her something to wear soon. She could still hear Lucille's clear voice, instructing her. *Ladies turn themselves out properly. We carry ourselves with decorum.*

Cole swung down from the horse, tying it to a post, and lifted her down roughly. Grabbing her by the arm, he marched her over to the horse that was trailing right behind them.

"Gotta check to be sure the trail ahead is clear," he growled. "You watch her." He released her arm and marched away.

An unfamiliar man stood in front of her. He had the

same swarthy skin, same nose, same broad shoulders as Cole. But unlike Cole, his dark beard was more scant, and his eyes... those eyes. They were piercing blue, unlike Cole's dark brown, and something about them sent a shiver down Aida's spine. Aida knew just from looking at the man's eyes there was nothing he was incapable of. Whereas Cole was implacable, this man was cruel.

"We're stopping to eat. Cole's dealing with an issue with the team, so you mind yourself. And unless you want to answer to him, you'll do as yer told. C'mere. We'll go sit by the clearin' and you'll help me cook." He pointed to a small clearing to the right, while her mind swirled. The man in front of her narrowed his eyes. "You have 'til the count of ten." She began to walk awkwardly, her battered backside protesting with each move as the man came to her side. His eyes trailed down the front of her thin chemise, and Aida felt suddenly naked. He grinned wickedly and licked his lips. His voice dropped to a low growl. "Cryin' shame Cole claimed you first. Ain't fair the older brother gets first pick'a the spoils. I could make you scream in pleasure just as soon as I'd have you screamin' in pain."

Aida tried to pull up the front of her dress, but it was fruitless with her wrists bound. She couldn't cover herself if she tried. He merely leered at her when she froze. The little hairs on her arms stood on end.

"You have five seconds," he spat out. Reluctantly, she closed the small gap between them, but when she did, he reached for her and to her horror, snagged her by the hair and planted his mouth on hers in a crude, rough kiss. Her hands still bound, she had no way to get away as she moved her head and his hand grasped the back of her hair. But just as soon as the kiss began, it stopped, and to her shock, the brute was pulled away.

Cole stood in front of her, lifting the man up by the back of his shirt. He spun him around and shoved him away. The younger man swore, but cringed as Cole glared with a ferocity Aida hadn't seen even during her punishment.

"You'll keep your fucking hands off her," Cole growled. He grabbed the man by the front of the shirt, lifting him right up on the tips of his toes. "You ever put your mouth on her again, I'll kill you."

Relief flooded through Aida as she righted herself. She reveled in the fear that flickered in the younger man's eyes as he nodded. But Cole wasn't done. Still holding the younger man by the front of his shirt, he hauled him over to where Aida was. "You tell her you're sorry."

"I'm sorry," the man muttered, clearly furious but afraid. Aida didn't respond, her mouth agape as she took the scene in. Was this some sort of game? Was she supposed to find Cole somehow more sympathetic? She'd heard of kidnappers playing such games, but found Cole's furious countenance unreadable.

"Go finish cookin'," Cole said, shoving him toward the fire. The other man shrugged his shoulders, as if to shake off what had just happened. Aida looked up at Cole, who slowly turned to her. He was still wearing his Stetson, which cast his dark eyes in shadow, but as he bent down to speak with her, his voice was softer than she'd yet heard. "Did he hurt you?" he asked. He placed a hand under her chin and met her eyes. He was probing. Aida was immediately struck by the difference between him and the man who'd assaulted her. But hadn't Cole just whipped her?

She shook her head. "No," she whispered.

Cole raked his eyes over her body, not the way the other man had, but as if to check her over. His jaw clenched. "You'll say, *no, sir,* or *no, Daddy.*"

She glared at him. "No, sir," she ground out.

Though his eyes narrowed, he nodded. "Very good. You need some privacy to visit the privy? And I've got a dress for you to change into. Wouldn't want you catchin' cold, darlin'."

"How thoughtful."

He lifted a stern brow. "I'll send Junior down to keep watch while you freshen up. Then you'll join us to eat," he said, his hand now upon her hip. She knew then that he meant to be sure she didn't get away.

"Junior!" Cole shouted. His hand felt warm on her skin. She wanted to hate him. But somehow, seeing him defend her from the threat of the other man made her soften, just a bit.

The young blond man came into view. "Yessir?"

"Take Aida down to the water to freshen herself up. Don't let her out of your sight, but," he paused, and turning to her, he raised a brow, "you gonna run?"

The two-second pause just before she shook her head was her mistake. His eyes narrowed. Of course she was going to run. What reason did she have to stay?

Cole's jaw clenched as he quickly made a decision. "On second thought, I think I'll escort her myself," he said. "You see to the team bein' watered, yeah?"

Junior nodded. "Yessir." He tipped his hat and went on his way, as Cole took Aida by the elbow and walked her down to the creek, muttering under his breath.

The air was warm and stagnant, and a gleam of perspiration dampened her chest as he escorted her. It wasn't until she was only a few feet away from the creek that she realized there was no 'privy.' She'd be expected to wash herself and take care of her duties with nothing more than cold water and leaves to dry herself off.

"I can't do this," she said, the ridiculous protestation sounding silly even to her own ears.

"What's that?" Cole said. He looked genuinely confused.

"You want me to *wash* in the *water*?" she asked. It seemed a horrendous option. "Have you no soap? Nothing to dry myself, or truly freshen up?"

He grinned, pulling a rough piece of cloth and foul-smelling slab of soap from his pocket. "Course I do, darlin'," he said. "You don't think we're a bunch of savages, now do you?" Something about his voice sent shivers along her spine, the implied meaning causing her stomach to clench. Of course they were savages.

She would have to make do.

"And when you're done here, you'll come back and eat with us. Doc makes a mean cornbread with beans, and there's plenty. You'll need your strength for the days ahead."

She *despised* beans, and only ever ate porridge or bread and butter with eggs at home, the food her cook placed upon dainty plates for her.

"I'm not hungry," she lied, her stomach growling in betrayal.

He laughed mirthlessly. "I didn't ask if you were hungry. I told you you were going to eat. Now, pretty girl, you have two choices," he said, as they came upon the edge of the creek. "You'll either do as I tell you," he paused, his voice dropping as he fixed her with a stern glare, "or disobey me and earn another trip over Daddy's knee. Understood?" He stopped walking and looked expectantly in her face. His eyes had hardened, his jaw set.

She swallowed, unable to swallow the fear that set her heart stuttering. "Fine," she hissed.

His hand shot out before she even knew what was happening, delivering a startling swat to her backside. "You watch that tone, young lady," he said, all teasing now gone from his eyes. "You'll respond properly with a *yes, Daddy*, or I'll spank your pretty bottom right here and now."

The *nerve*!

She pursed her lips but truly did not want to be punished again. She had no doubt he meant what she said. She inhaled, keeping her anger in check with considerable difficulty. "Yes, Daddy," she nearly growled.

He grinned. "Good girl. Now go take care of business, and remember what happens to naughty girls who don't obey their daddies. Go, now," he said, pointing to the creek. Silently cursing him out, she obeyed.

CHAPTER FOUR

Love me or hate me, both are in my favor. — *William Shakespeare*

Cole watched her choke down the food she no doubt despised, while she glared at him. He narrowed his eyes at her and took a large bite, chewing quickly. They couldn't stay for long, and had to get moving on the trail. Out of the corner of his eye, he took in Junior, who was piling the dirty dishes together ready to be washed, and his brother Justice, who was brooding on the side, watching all that went down. His brother had always been unpredictable and cruel, which served him well in their posse. But for the first time, Cole began to fear that his brother's character threatened the girl. Justice had kept his amorous pursuits hidden from Cole, but he'd heard rumors. Now Cole wondered exactly what he was capable of.

"You need more, darlin'?" Cole asked, but the question was scornful, not kind.

"No," she hissed.

He narrowed his eyes and wagged a finger. "You mind yourself, pretty girl. I'm only makin' sure you've got plenty in your belly before we mosey on." She pursed her lips as he took another bite of bread. "Now, it seems to me I've been remiss. You ain't been properly introduced to the rest of our company."

He pointed a lazy finger at Justice, who sat furthest away from the group. His brooding eyes met Cole's as he spoke. "Justice, my younger brother, fastest gunslinger in our company, fearless." *And unpredictable*, he thought grimly to himself, remembering how badly he'd wanted to knock his brother's teeth down his throat when he'd had the nerve to touch her. He wasn't sure what angered him more: the fact that his brother'd crossed a line and attempted to assault Aida, or his own anger that rose up in her defense. It wouldn't do to grow soft when he had a mission to accomplish. Not at all. Justice nodded. "You two have met," Cole said, barely tempering a growl. Aida, to her credit, was unmoved.

"Over here's Doc," Cole said, as Aida reluctantly followed his gesture. Doc was Cole's age, a widower in his early twenties, an educated man who'd turned to darker ways when he lost his wife to murder six months after they had wed. He was invaluable as a healer in their group, when gunshot wounds, illness, and disease threatened them. He was also the brains of the group. Tall, with thick brown hair, blue eyes, and spectacles, Doc appeared to be every bit the gentleman and scholar. But Cole well knew what he was capable of, and relied on him when the chips were down.

"Pleased to meet you," Doc said, tipping his hat to Aida. She gave the slightest nod of her head, but her gaze did not soften.

"You've met Junior," Cole said, pointing another finger at the young blond, who grinned at her while he cleaned his fingernails with the tip of a dagger. Maybe Aida could be tricked into trusting him.

"Howdy," Junior said. Aida's eyes softened just the slightest bit. Lucky for Junior he looked innocent. Cole used that to the advantage of his posse on more than one occasion.

"Last of the crew," he said, pointing a final finger to

Preach, shorter but heftier than Cole. Though he was a dependable member of their crew, he held fast to select morals. He had a shock of black hair, piercing brown eyes, a heavy beard, and a well-fed belly. He lifted his bowl to his lips and finished the rest of his beans before lifting a hand to his temple and saluting Aida as Cole introduced him. "Preach. If we need a man with morals, we draw on him," Cole said, eliciting snickers from the rest of the men and a grin from Preach. The truth was, Preach was the brawn of the group. Having lost his betrothed in a bar brawl in his youth, he'd turned to religion before he'd turned to their dark ways. He was fearless and brutally strong.

"And now, darlin'," Cole said. "Why don't you introduce yourself."

She shoved a corner of cornbread in her mouth and glared silently. Cole clenched his jaw. It'd been less than twenty-four hours since he'd thrashed her, but she was cruising for another trip over his knee before the sun set. He placed his bowl down and pushed himself to standing. Maybe if he bared her bottom in front of the other men, she'd think twice about defiance. But watching him prepare to advance on her, her eyes widened slightly, and she swallowed her bread.

"Aida Perkins," she said. "And I've no doubt you all know who I am, or you wouldn't have taken me from my home."

Cole winked at her. "You catch on quickly there, darlin'," he drawled. "But let's hear who you are from your own lips. Who's your daddy?" As the words left his mouth, he felt the reminder in his gut. Some would call him a sick bastard, but he loved making her call him Daddy. It made her squirm, and made his cock harden to see her reluctance to say the name. *Daddy.*

"George Perkins," Aida said, lifting her chin defiantly. "Owns the ranch you all raided, and I'm his only daughter." To Cole's surprise, she offered no more information, and as she spoke of her father, her jaw clenched. There was something behind her shuttered eyes that looked like barely contained hatred. There was a reason why they'd been sent for her. He'd uncover that reason.

"Excellent," Cole said, drawing himself to his full height as he turned to face them all. "We leave shortly, move as quickly as we can while the light of day shines. We should reach our destination by nightfall."

To his surprise, Aida spoke up. "And where is your destination?" she asked.

He merely smiled at her and cocked his head. "Well now, darlin'," he said. "I can't be givin' too many of our secrets away, now can I?" He sobered, his voice dropping, as he walked over to her and the men got busy clearing their dishes and preparing to move on. He leaned down and whispered in her ear, "No need for you to worry about any of that. You just keep your eyes on me and do as you're told, yeah?"

Though her lips were pursed and her eyes gleamed, she nodded. But they all froze, as seconds later, the sound of a horse's hooves pounding in their direction caught their attention. Aida got to her feet. Cole grabbed her arm lest she thought to take advantage of the distraction and make a run for it. But she stood as still as he did.

CHAPTER FIVE

I desire the things which will destroy me in the end. — Sylvia Plath

The pounding of a horse's hooves halted as a large steed came into view. Aida's hand involuntarily went to her chest, though she stayed stock still with Cole's hand on her elbow. She blinked, surprised that the rider was a woman not much older than herself, with a strange swath of fabric tied to her back. The woman had been riding hard, her eyes wide with terror, as she came to a halt.

"Help me!" she screamed. The men in the party looked at her in shock. Cole leaned close to Aida and whispered, "You run, I will catch you, and make that whipping I gave you look like child's play." She hadn't thought of running, so intent was she on hearing what terrified the poor woman in front of her, but his hissed warning scared her nonetheless. She nodded. Cole released her and stepped up to the woman.

"Tell me why you need help."

Aida looked quickly at the other men around her. Justice was unmoved, his cold eyes calculating, but Junior's hand was on his gun, Doc had stood and now his arms were on his chest, and Preach was standing in a sort of half-crouching position, as if ready to pounce. These men had kidnapped Aida and she'd been treated brutally, but they were not unmoved by a damsel in distress. Aida watched, fascinated.

"It's my husband," the woman said. "He's after me. He's half-crazed, says I had an affair with another man. I never did, never!" she said. Her wide eyes seemed contrite. "I merely had a neighbor help me when my husband was traveling. He said he would kill me, and I ran. I've been riding hard to get to my kinfolk over the river, hoping they'd help me. I thought I'd gotten away, but he's found me."

Aida's breath caught in her throat as the sound of pounding hooves again reached her ears. The men sprang into action. Cole reached his hands for the woman, pulling her down from the horse. He swore aloud as the mysterious fabric on her back squirmed and let out a cry.

"Lord have mercy, it's a baby," Preach muttered in his deep, growly voice. Aida gasped as Cole grabbed the woman roughly and shoved her over to Aida.

"You two get behind Preach," he growled. Aida stood frozen to the spot. Cole reached for her arm and half-shoved her over to Preach. "*Now!*"

Aida stumbled but obeyed, her arm protectively out to the woman. Preach stood guard in front, as Justice drew his weapon and Junior's eyes narrowed to mere slits. Doc watched all with calculating eyes.

Seconds later, a second rider came into view, dark hair beneath his hat making him look menacing, a look of fury across his face as he spied the woman.

"You think you've found someone to save you, do you?" the man said, ignoring the onlookers. "You've done me wrong, and I'll see you pay for it."

The woman screamed and got behind Aida. Once again, Aida instinctively put her arms out to protect the woman and her baby. It seemed the man was unshaken by witnesses, and the woman's fears were not unwarranted. To Aida's horror, the man reached to his belt and withdrew a pistol. Quick rustles and five clicks sounded at once, as the man faced Cole's entire crew, each of whom was pointing a pistol at the man.

"No man'll pull a gun on a woman on my watch," Cole said in the same no-nonsense voice he'd used to tell Aida to get to cover. "Drop your weapon, or I'll kill you. You've got 'til the count of three to drop it 'fore I give my men leave to fire. One…"

The man's eyes were wild and crazed as his hand shook, pointing the gun first at all of them. Aida's heart pounded so that she felt strangled by fear, her ability to move or even think frozen on the spot.

"Two," Cole said, louder this time, and the man still held his gun. Now would be the moment.

"Three." The man moved to shoot, but shots rang out as Aida pulled the woman to the ground, covering her with her own body, careful not to harm the baby. She could hear shouts and more shots, a sound of a scuffle. Curse words were uttered, and another shot that had a ring of finality to it. Then everything was quiet. She stayed right where she was, panting, while the woman beneath her lay stock still. Had she been shot? In the silence, the wails of a baby rose loud and strong.

"My baby," the woman whispered. "Lord have mercy, is he all right?" Aida dared to lift her head just a little, and as she lifted her head, her eyes met Cole's dark gaze. She gasped, jumping up.

"Your husband's dead," Cole told the woman simply. "Stand up."

Instead of reaching for Aida's hand, Cole put both arms around her waist and hoisted her to her feet, glancing over her body with pursed lips and narrowed eyes. "You unharmed?" he growled.

"Y-yessir," Aida stammered, confused as to why he was checking to see if she was unharmed when a woman with a child had been just as vulnerable. Preach came to them in three large strides, his enormous hands gentle as he reached to the woman's back and ever so gently extracted the baby, his growly voice crooning as he hushed it. But Cole hadn't left Aida's side. His eyes roamed her body, hands probing to see if she had, indeed, been unharmed. His large, strong hand grasped her elbow, and Aida was reminded that she was no willing member of their party, but a captive.

"Take the body," Cole barked out to Justice and Junior. "Drag it to the river. You know the routine. Take any money and give it to the woman, any weapons we keep for ourselves." He turned to Preach. "Check the horse for injury and bring 'em here." To Doc, he said, "You check her and the baby over." The men sprang into action, and Aida watched, mesmerized as Cole gave his final instructions. "Leave the body face down, where he's unlikely to be found until the face is unrecognizable. Clean well, cover your tracks, and come back here as quickly as you can."

Clearly, they'd done this before. Likely many times.

It wasn't until Cole's arm went around her shoulders that she realized she was trembling so badly her teeth clattered together. When his mouth came to her ear and whispered, "Hush now, darlin'. You're all right, and no harm will come to you," she noticed the trembling began to lessen. She wondered at first if his tender side was just a show for the woman, so she'd trust him, but the woman was off with Doc, and Cole and Aida were nearly alone. Still, she would not, *could* not soften, even now.

"I'm fine, thank you," she said, attempting to pull away from him. He merely gave her a sidelong glance and held on tighter.

"You be a good girl, and you *will* be fine," he replied. Given the choice to fight and provoke him or pretend to comply, it seemed the best option was feigned submission.

If feigning submission was what would help her get to safety and freedom, she'd put on her best show.

She bowed her head and whispered, "Yes, sir."

The grip on her elbow did not slacken.

CHAPTER SIX

One need not be a chamber to be haunted. — *Emily Dickinson*

Cole watched his men assemble in front of him.

"And what do we do with the woman and baby?" Justice said, a lip curling, glaring at Cole as if somehow he was responsible for their larger party. "She got a name?"

"Patricia," Cole said.

Justice frowned. "We've no time for this bullshit, and another woman and a baby in our group'll complicate things." Justice had no use for those weaker than himself, unless it was to use a whore to his advantage. He was brief, he was cruel, and he moved on. To him, expending effort protecting them was a preposterous notion.

"Drop 'em by the river and let them fend for themselves," Junior said, his lips pursed with sarcasm. "Is that what you'd have us do?" Junior's penchant for pretty ladies would harm them one day, Cole was sure of it. His brother's ruthless nature was far more useful in their line of work.

Justice made a move to advance on Junior and Junior turned to face him. Cole held out a hand, prepared to pull them off each other and beat the tar out of both of them if they fought.

"Enough." They knew not to push him. Both men froze, glaring at each other.

"She said her family's nearby, no?" Preach said. All eyes turned to him. "She's got kin just over the river," he said. "We'll be behind in our plans if we all go deliver her, but I can escort her. Won't be but a half day's journey. I'll meet y'all up at Lawson's mornin' after next."

Cole shook his head. "Not sure it's right to split," he said, removing his tobacco pouch from his pocket.

"What other choice do we have?" Preach asked. "Leave a woman with a baby? You know me, Cole. I'll bust the nose of any man I need to, and just as soon pump iron into a man deservin' of it as I would pick my teeth after dinner, but I won't be party to abandonin' a woman and child."

Justice glared at him and spat on the ground furiously. God, Cole had to get him hooked up with a woman of the line the next town up. He had to calm the hell down.

Cole gave a curt nod. "We can't all go together," he said. "That much is true. Seems there's one bad choice and a worse one on the table here." He cursed, kicking the toe of his boot in the dirt while he took a tug on his cigarette. Slowly exhaling the smoke in wispy tendrils, he narrowed his eyes on Aida and Patricia. The women spoke to one another in hushed whispers. Cole frowned. It wouldn't do to have Aida telling her anything about their group. He'd allowed them to stay together to keep them quiet, but now he wondered. If Patricia knew she'd been kidnapped... But before he met with his men, he'd threatened Aida with another whipping, warning her not to tell Patricia the truth. If she responded to fear, then fear would be his ally. And she knew he was a man of his word. As he glanced over at her, she tucked in a blanket around the sleeping baby. After the commotion, the infant squalled loud enough to wake the dead, but Patricia had quickly hushed him with feeding and rocking. Now the two women and baby sat at a distance while the men convened.

If Aida obeyed, now would be the time to turn on his charm. Fear, then feigned kindness, would ensure her submission. He might even earn her loyalty, if played right.

He glanced back over at Patricia. Preach was offering to take her to her family, but Preach was an integral part of his play. The timing could work out well. He ran a finger along the stubble on his jaw as he mulled everything over.

Cole scowled. "All right, Preach," he said. "You take the woman and baby. You leave her with her kin, and you hightail it back to where we're supposed to meet." He paused before continuing. "You know what's at stake if you don't meet us at Lawson's."

Junior swore. Doc scowled, and Justice looked ready to spit nails. Preach knew exactly where they were supposed to meet. The plans had been in place for months. Preach nodded his assent, though, and the men disassembled as Cole and Preach finalized plans.

As night began to fall, Cole instructed Doc to get dinner going. "You be sure you cook those beans as well, yeah?" he asked. He wanted Doc to cook foods Aida didn't like. He would train her. She would hate him in the end, but he was going to give it his best shot. The woman would learn to obey.

• • • • • • •

As night fell, Cole instructed his men to quit their jobs and get some rest. They spread out their bedrolls, the woman and baby at the furthest end of their company, Junior on one side and Doc the other. Preach stood sentry for the first night watch. Justice would be up next, and Cole would take the shift at daybreak. It was time for Cole to put the next part of his plan into action.

Aida was sitting apart from the rest, righting her hair and frowning, clearly uncomfortable with the thought of another night sleeping on the hard ground, removed from her vanity mirror and precious pampering tools. Cole's lips twitched. She certainly had been jolted out of what was comfortable and familiar. He hoped her being uncomfortable would make his next plans work well. He ambled over to her and crouched down.

"How you doin', darlin'?" he asked, trying his best to appear truly concerned for her. She shifted and looked up at him, shrugging, but didn't answer.

Lowering his voice and raising his eyebrows slightly, he leaned in. "Aida, when I ask you a question, I expect an answer."

Her eyes glanced side to side before she whispered, "Fine." She turned away from him. This wouldn't do at all.

"Night's growin' cold, darlin'," he murmured. "You'll share a bedroll with me tonight."

Her eyes widened, then narrowed in anger. "I wouldn't share a bedroll with you if I were freezing to death!"

Leaning closer to her, he took her chin in his hand. "I didn't ask you, sweetheart. Now you go right yourself for bed and strip to your chemise. I'll prepare our bed, and you'll join me."

"I will not," she hissed.

Cole was unmoved. Leaning in close, he whispered in her ear, "I don't care who's in our company or if it's night or day. You defy me and I'll whip you. Is that what you want Daddy to do? Strip you and paddle your bare bottom? What will the others say?"

"They'll say you're a brute," she whispered back.

His plan was not working. Though he was certainly prepared to whip her—and suspected she'd land herself over his knee before the week was out—this strategy wouldn't be as effective given the next leg of their journey. He tried a different tactic.

Reaching a hand out, he gently encircled her neck and drew her close to him. He might've been rough with her, but women were not immune to his seduction. He flexed his fingers on the back of her neck, massaging, as he whispered in his deepest voice, "Aida, we got off on the wrong foot. I spanked you for defyin' me, and I'll do it again if I have to. But I don't want to punish you." It was a lie. His cock twitched with the mere thought of taking his hand to her bare bottom. "But you must obey me for your own good." His voice dropped lower. "You've had a long day, darlin'. You be a good girl now, and do as you're told. You may even find if you obey me, I treat good girls very nicely."

He could see her begin to soften when her breath became more shallow and her eyelids fluttered. Still, she pursed her lips as she glared at him. "Fine," she hissed.

He tsk-tsked. "Try again, darlin'."

She closed her eyes, inhaled, then blurted out, "Yes, Daddy."

"Good girl," he crooned. "Now strip." The last command was said low, not forcefully, but in a way that commanded her attention.

She glanced nervously around her, stood and walked to a nearby tree. Hurriedly, she stripped her clothing until she stood near him wearing nothing but her chemise. He'd already assembled their bedroll, and while she'd prepared herself, he'd removed his boots, belt, and Stetson. A few minutes later, he lifted the blanket and gestured for her to join him.

"Come, now," he ordered.

She closed her eyes briefly before she obeyed. As she lay beside him, she was rigid, holding her body apart from him as best as she could in their confined quarters.

"Relax now, honey," he said. "We got off to a rough start, but you'll see I'm not all that bad if you can trust me. Relax. I promise I won't take advantage of you."

He smoothed a hand over her hip, soothing, ignoring the uncomfortable tightening in his pants. If his plan was going to work, she'd have to trust him. "I'll not hurt you," he said. "That's not my style. I don't enjoy taking advantage of women against their will." That was his brother's specialty, and partly why Aida was sharing his bedroll. "Sleep now, honey."

So far, he'd shown her he was a man of his word. He'd done what he said, every time. And yes, he'd been rough and he'd spanked her. He would do it again if he had to. But if he could only get her to trust him…

He lifted a hand and ever so gently trailed his fingers through her hair, starting at the scalp and carefully moving down to her neck. At first, she tensed, but he whispered, "Shhh. You've had a rough day. You relax now," moving his hands through her hair over and over again. After a time, he rested his hand back on her hip, a gesture of protection and comfort. Finally, the tension seeped out of her shoulders. Her body relaxed against his, and moments later, he heard her steady breathing. She was asleep.

He smiled to himself. He was good at this, so good he almost believed it himself.

CHAPTER SEVEN

Courage is knowing what not to fear. — Plato

Aida woke at the crack of dawn, Cole's hand still resting upon her hip. She'd never been touched by a man like this before, and she hated that her body betrayed her. She wanted to despise the man who'd taken her and whipped her. But despite her best effort to do so, he kept making her change her mind. It wasn't fair.

The way his voice had soothed her, low and commanding but not overbearing, had made her body relax despite her best effort not to fall for his seduction. She'd wanted to hate his hand stroking through her hair, but her body had had other ideas. He was so strong and handsome, and she had never known the touch of a man like him before. She'd ignored the voice in her mind that had warned her against trusting him and had reveled in the peace she felt. And she had been exhausted. She'd felt his hardness against her backside as they lay together, but the fact that his hand had never moved beyond her hip, never grasped her breasts or touched between her legs, somehow convinced her that maybe he really wasn't a vicious or loathsome man. There were others in their party who were vicious. But perhaps he wasn't one of them. He was feared. He was the leader.

Though Cole had taken her, he'd said it was to teach her father a lesson. And didn't her father need a lesson! The mere thought of her father getting a taste of what he deserved thrilled her. And though Cole had whipped her, he'd defended her against his brother, and killed a man who had threatened to hurt Patricia.

Maybe Cole wasn't all that bad.

As she struggled with her conscience, her mind went back to something Lucille had once told her. "Sometimes those who should love us don't. And those who shouldn't do." What a strange thing to think, she thought to herself, pursing her lips. Cole certainly didn't love her. He very likely hated her.

Cole's hand flexed on her hip. "You awake, Aida?" he asked.

Shifting away from him, she sat up. "Yes," she said shortly. Her stomach rolled with hunger. Her eyes were gritty with sleep, and she was in desperate need of a bath. How she missed the claw-footed bath at home, her thick slab of fragrant soap, her ivory-handled comb and mirror. If she got out of this unscathed, she'd never take her pampering for granted again. All she needed was a hot bath and a clean dress. She'd have neither.

"Up we go, then. Go get dressed," Cole ordered, as if she really needed direction. Now that the others were rising, the first thing she needed to do was get dressed and ready.

Scrambling out of the bedroll, she grabbed the folded clothing she'd left nearby. As she lifted her clothes, something skittered across her hand. She let out a scream that could be heard for miles. Her heart hammered in her chest, and she grew faint from fright. An enormous spider had climbed atop her clothing and was scrambling over her. Cole wasted no time. He slapped his hand out, the spider falling to the ground, as he lifted his boot and crushed it.

"You see that red dot?" he said grimly. "Poisonous.

Otherwise I'd not have killed it."

She barely heard his words, though, as her eyes were clamped shut, the blood ringing in her ears. She hated spiders. Always had, always would. She was terrified of their creepy-crawly legs, pincers, and mouths, and never could even summon neutral appreciation for the tamest. She hated all manner of spider. She swayed, her legs wobbling beneath her, still feeling the shock of terror and fear shoot tremors through her body. She was vaguely aware of Cole coming closer, as she swallowed hard to avoid crying. Crying over the spider would be embarrassing, though her throat was tight and her nose stung. To her surprise, she felt Cole's arms wrap around her.

"You all right, sweetheart?" he asked in her ear. She merely shook her head, not trusting herself to speak. He pulled her to his chest, and though she wanted to protest, she did not. He was strong, and despite being on the trail, he smelled nice, the sweet, pungent scent of tobacco mingling with leather. She'd never been held like this, in the arms of a strong man, and it was not unpleasant. He gently placed a kiss atop her head.

"You're gonna be okay there, pretty girl. The spider's gone and I'm here."

Oh, how she wished she could trust his words. It pained her to have to put her guard back up. Despite how lovely it felt in his arms, she pushed herself away.

"I'm fine, thank you," she said. Cole released her, but held her at arm's length, his dark eyes penetrating hers.

"You sure you're okay?" he asked low. Others in their party had glanced at her, but now moved on, as everyone was busy preparing to move on.

She nodded. Time to play submissive again. "Yes, sir," she whispered. If she could only get him to think she was obedient, when they reached the next town, opportunity might arise. "I'm fine."

He nodded, appeased, and kissed her forehead gently, his whiskers tickling. To her dismay, her heart fluttered again. "Good girl," he murmured. "Now go on and get dressed. I don't want anyone's eyes seein' you dressed like this but mine."

She wondered why he cared now how she was dressed, when she'd been hauled out of her house in front of all of them in nothing but a chemise?

He spun her around and gave her a teasing swat, sending her on her way. Her cheeks burned in embarrassment, not just from the realization that she was only dressed in her chemise, but because her body had betrayed her, the force of the gentle swat making heat pulse between her legs. Angry tears filled her eyes. She had to hate him. She simply had to.

CHAPTER EIGHT

Pain and pleasure, like light and darkness, succeed each other. — Laurence Sterne

They rode a full day, stopping only for a brief meal Cole allowed. He watched Aida reluctantly choke down hardtack with coffee. She was learning. Patricia fed her baby, and explained that an Indian woman she'd befriended taught her how to tie her baby to her back. It was a useful tool, as the baby dozed easily while they rode hard. Patricia sat behind Preach, holding tightly to his large body, and when they stopped, Preach saw to her needs. He hoped Preach wasn't growing soft on her. Any attachment to a woman on the trail was dangerous.

Aida rode behind him, at the head of the pack, holding onto him. It seemed she held on less reluctantly than when they first began, and he hoped it would stay that way. Time would tell.

The clomping of horse's hooves came beside him, until Justice rode next to him. "You reckon we'll make it to Lawson's in time?" he asked.

Cole clenched his jaw and nodded. They were not to speak of their plans in front of Aida. "You know it," he growled. They'd ride hard all night if they had to but his plans would not fail. "Everything's workin' just as it should, except for yesterday, but we ain't slowed down none. Now no more talk of it."

Justice gave a barely perceptible nod, gently lifting the reins on his horse so that she slowed and fell in line behind Cole.

"We're going to Litchfield?" Aida asked behind him.

Cole swore. Curse his brother and his claptrap. Women didn't have the faintest sense of direction and she likely wouldn't have even known where they were otherwise.

"That's the plan, darlin'," he said, with forced gentleness. "You feelin' all right back there?"

"Mmm," she answered. "Need to use the facilities soon," she said. "When we get to Litchfield?"

He swore under his breath. "Don't say the name of the town aloud again, Aida," he ordered. "Best we keep that secret. And we're due for a stop, so we'll pull over at the clearin' and water the horses. You can visit the privy then."

She muttered under her breath, and he gave her a sidelong glance. She quieted.

"Hold!" Cole shouted, holding up a hand. The party came to a stop, as Cole swung down from the horse. "Last stop before we reach our first destination for the night. Up ahead lies the railroad station. We leave Preach and Patricia in town, then move on to where we'll sleep tonight. Anyone need to relieve themselves or get some water, do it now. I'll give you fifteen minutes. I want everyone back here promptly."

Murmurs came back to him, "Yes, sir," and "You've got it, boss," as the men stretched their legs and secured their horses. Aida began to walk away.

"And where do you think you're goin'?" Cole asked, trotting to keep up with her.

"To use the facilities," she said. Her eyes flashed at him as she lifted her skirts up over the leaves. It was no use. They were already caked with dust from the trail, and dragging on the ground. Holding her skirts was likely habit. She continued to walk ahead of him.

"You wait for me," he ordered, but she didn't slow. In two large strides he caught up with her, took her by the elbow, and delivered a sharp swat. "I said wait up for me, young lady."

She froze, her chin lifted high, stock still. "Fine." She'd obey, but not happily. Someone was looking to get her pretty little backside blistered.

He marched her to the creek, no longer allowing her to have the illusion of freedom, but holding her steady. Soon, when they were alone in a hotel room in Lawson's, he'd turn on the charm again. But right now, his instincts to make her obey were in full force.

When they reached the water's edge, she turned and asked him to leave her be.

"One minute," he said, lifting a finger in warning. "One, and I'll be back."

He turned his back to her to give her privacy, counting slowly in his head, listening for any signs of escape. But he could hear her right behind him. She was not running. When he reached sixty, he turned to her. She was just finishing righting herself, when a flash of silver caught his eye. She gasped, but it was too late. The pistol fell from her waist and to the ground.

"Freeze," Cole growled. "Don't you move a goddamn muscle."

Her eyes looked up at him, wide and fearful as he prowled closer. Junior's pistol, red-handled and unmistakable, lay at the ground at her feet. Cole picked it up and glanced it over.

"Well, well, little lady, what have we here?" he said. "When did you come about this little stolen piece of property?"

She cast her eyes at the ground and refused to speak.

He took one step closer and reached for her, her entire delicate chin engulfed in his large hand. "You've already earned yourself a trip over Daddy's knee for stealin', little girl," he said. "Now fess up before Daddy's forced to punish you more severely."

She swallowed, and fear tripped across her features. She jerked her face from his hand, looking away as she spoke. "This morning at breakfast," she mumbled. "He left it out because he'd cleaned it. I took it then and hid it."

Cole glared. Not only had she stolen the gun, now he'd have to deal with Junior. Likely Junior hadn't told him about the missing weapon because he feared being punished himself. Cole had few laws in his band, but one of them was a man must be armed at all times. Losing one's weapon was a major infraction, and couldn't go unpunished.

He nodded once. "I'll deal with Junior later," he growled. "I'll deal with you now."

She took one step back before he grasped her arm firmly, marching her over to a fallen tree. He turned her to face him.

"You're getting a spanking, Aida. You know that, don't you, little girl?" Her eyes flitted away, but a quick chuck of his finger under her chin brought her glance back to his. "Do you think Daddy can let sneaking go unpunished?" He made his voice intentionally gentle but firm, his tone scolding but kind. "I don't want you hurt, honey," he said softly. "A big ol' gun like that could hurt you. And Daddy needs to teach you a lesson to keep you safe." He sat, drawing her firmly across his knees. It surprised him how little resistance she gave.

He slowly raised her skirts. He'd taken many women across his knee, and he well knew the intimate touch like this could work in his favor. He wasn't truly angry with her. He was almost proud of her courage and tenacity. And she'd acted the part of the chastened girl quite well, to his immense pleasure. His cock hardened at her rounded bottom over his knee, her perfect figure begging to be touched. His hand went to the front of her drawers and he tugged the drawstring. Her hand flew back but he deftly pinned it.

"Hands down, young lady," he said sternly.

She kicked her feet in protest as he lowered her drawers. He gave her one sharp swat to the crease of her thighs and bottom. She yelped.

"Daddy told you what would happen if you misbehaved. A good bare-bottom spanking should make my point loud and clear." He pulled her drawers down while she begged him to stop. Determined, he pulled them down to her knees and rested his hand on her naked bottom. God, he wanted to take her.

"Why is Daddy spanking you, little girl?" he asked.

Her shoulders slumped. "I took the gun," she whispered.

"Was that honest?" he asked.

She shook her head vehemently, as he ran his hand from the small of her back to the top of her thighs.

"No," he said softly. "Now, we can't have dishonesty between us, young lady. What you did was not only dishonest and disobedient, but you also risked injury to yourself. And I can't allow that to happen."

He lifted his hand and brought it down sharply on her naked skin. She yelled out loud. He felt the satisfying sting in his hand as he administered a second sound swat. The loud clap of his hand on her bottom resounded in the quiet. Again, he spanked her and this time her little feet kicked in protest.

"None of that, now, darlin'," he said firmly, while delivering a handful of rapid swats to the place just below her bottom, where it stung worse than ever. She whimpered, but he continued spanking.

"I'll not have you put yourself in danger," he said, lifting his hand and administering another hard stroke. Her bottom was growing red now. His cock ached. She wiggled, and his hand around her waist firmed. "You obey Daddy, and you won't find yourself like this again," he said, giving her several more punishing swats. "Getting your pretty little bottom tanned over Daddy's knee."

She moaned, but he continued. His cock throbbed, desire consuming him every time his hand connected with her beautiful backside.

"Daddy wants to treat you well," Cole continued. "And not have to take you across his knee to be spanked like a naughty little girl. But if you disobey, this is where you'll be, sweetheart." Another sharp swat followed another, until she was flaming hot to the touch, her backside a sunset crimson. He closed his eyes briefly. She was so beautiful. If only…

He stopped spanking her, running his hand over her punished bottom. "Has Daddy made his point, darlin'?" he asked.

She nodded.

"Good girl," he crooned. "Such a good girl, taking her spanking over Daddy's knee." Slowly, he dipped his middle finger between her legs, a slow, wicked grin spreading across his face when he found her slick with arousal. She wiggled in protest.

"Ohh," she said. "Oh, please don't!" He guessed her face was as flushed as her vulnerable bottom spread over his lap.

"Just relax, honey," he whispered. "You took your spanking like such a good girl. Now let Daddy make it a little better." This time she didn't protest as his fingers traveled between her legs. First, he explored her core. Gently, he pushed his fingers on the inside of her thighs. "Open up wide, sweetheart," he coaxed. To his immense pleasure, she obeyed. His chest tightened along with his cock as he slowly plunged a finger between her legs again.

"That's a girl," he crooned. As slowly as possible, he carefully slid his finger to her sensitive nub, circling in firm but gentle strokes. He lowered his head and whispered, "Does that feel nice, darlin'? I'll not hurt you. Trust Daddy and take what's yours. You took your punishment. Now take your reward. Such a good girl," he crooned as she squirmed on his lap.

One hand released her waist and gently brushed across her chest until he felt what he was looking for. Her hardened nipples. Oh, this would do quite well. He gently lowered his hand beneath the top of her dress until his fingers grasped a nipple. He squeezed, while at the same time flicking his finger over her nub. Over and over again he teased her nipple and stroked her, all the while whispering to her. "Just relax," he said. "It's natural to feel excited now." He was not new to this exchange of power. Women loved his strength and dominance, growing weak in the knees and wet between the legs when he overpowered them. His fingers nimbly pinched her nipples so that she gasped, stroking her pussy until her back arched and she moaned.

"Good girl," he said, as she jerked beneath his hands. "Come for Daddy." She groaned and bucked, writhing as she climaxed hard. He continued to stroke her, easing back gently as she slowed, until she lay completely spent over his knee.

He released her, turning her over so that she lay in his arms. Her cheeks were bright red, as he'd suspected they would be, but as he drew her close to his chest, her arms reached for him.

"Hush now," he crooned. "You're a good girl. What a very good girl." He held her until she was breathing steadily, calm again, then he planted a kiss on her forehead and stood her up. "Now, little girl, I want it clear. You know why I spanked you?"

She nodded, swallowing, as he continued. "And you know that little bit at the end was your reward for taking your punishment like a good girl?"

Though her eyes cast down, she nodded again.

"Very good. Will you obey Daddy like a good girl now?"

Her eyes were softer when she looked at him. Could they be... trusting?

"Yes, Daddy," she whispered.

He could've shouted with glee. It was almost too easy.

CHAPTER NINE

Long is the way and hard, that leads out of Hell to light. — John Milton

Patricia leaned in and gave Aida an impulsive hug before she left. Aida kissed the woman's cheek and traced her hand on the tiny head of her sleeping baby, her hand trembling a bit. It both unnerved and panicked Aida that the only woman in their company was leaving, before Aida had even had a chance to get to know her. She hadn't confided a thing to her, and Patricia would likely remember Aida and her 'husband,' as well as the rest of the crew, fondly.

At her home, she'd mourned the loss of her tutor and friend, Lucille, though she hated to think of Lucille seeing her now. But it was when she was alone like this, in the quiet of night, or on the endless hours upon horseback, that she remembered with fondness Lucille's soft laugh and sweet instructions. Aida's mother had died at childbirth, and Lucille had been the only woman Aida had ever known as mother and friend.

Sadness descended on her as Patricia took her leave. The irony burned. The very men who'd taken her had rescued the woman who now roamed free.

Cole and Preach had a hushed conversation before Preach walked away. The large man heaved Patricia up on his own saddle, behind him, so she held tightly as he picked up the reins. Aida did her best to feel nothing. Allowing herself to feel numb emotionally was a skill she'd learned long before she'd ever met Cole.

She watched as Cole came back to their small group, his hands hitched in his pockets as his dark eyes darted back and forth, from one side to the next, taking it all in. Her heart thumped in her chest. It infuriated her that her body refused to submit to her angry protestations. *No*, she didn't want to feel safe when his arms wrapped around her at night. *No*, it wasn't right that being intimately strewn over his lap had felt darkly erotic. What kind of a woman was aroused by being spanked so harshly? How could she have let him bring her to ecstasy over his knee, the man who'd *taken* her from her home, an outlaw running from the law? The man who'd *whipped* her? It was wrong, so very wrong. Yet when he came to her side and his warm, rough hand engulfed hers, she stepped instinctively closer to him. He squeezed her hand, then held on tightly as he gestured for her to hoist herself up on his saddle. He followed suit.

"Y'all know what awaits us at the next stop," he said, as he rounded his horse and his dark eyes took in each one of his men. "I want every one of you focused on my instructions. You know the next town over who we meet, and y'all know it ain't unlikely our faces are plastered on *Wanted* posters. You know what to do. You know where we meet if we get split." He paused. "You know where your allegiance lies."

His speech left more questions than answers.

You all know.

She sure as hell didn't know. What did her father owing them money have to do with heading into the next town? She didn't realize she was looking at Cole questioningly until his dark eyes met hers and warmed. Leaning close enough to her so that she could smell the leather and smoke that'd become a familiar scent, he whispered in her ear, "You don't worry about instructions, honey. You keep your eyes on Daddy."

Daddy.

She clenched her jaw and looked straight ahead, giving a small nod to show she'd heard him, furious that her heart tripped in her chest and her body pulsed with heat. "Simply perfect," she muttered, now overcome with anger that Patricia and Preach were gone and she was left hopelessly attracted to a sadistic son of a bitch who made her call him Daddy. Excellent.

Cole gave her a sideways glance over his shoulder. "Sarcasm doesn't suit you, Aida." His voice dropped as he leaned back and whispered, "Careful, darlin'. You know what happens to naughty girls."

She swallowed hard, willing herself to remain aloof and detached and *not aroused* by his overt display of raw masculinity and power. He raised an eyebrow, she feigned obedience, nodding. His jaw clenched in reluctant approval as he pricked his spurs, their horse taking off at a gallop.

They rode hard into the night, stopping only for a brief spell to eat. She'd become accustomed to eating what she was served, under Cole's stern, watchful eye, but the griddle cakes caught in her throat, dry and unpalatable. At home, she'd never been forced to eat what she didn't like, and her father had fired chefs who hadn't accommodated her particular tastes.

"I'm not hungry anymore," she'd insisted, but she'd eaten hardly anything. She got to her feet, but he quickly took her by the elbow, bent her over, and gave her a good, hard swat. The other men hadn't even flinched, but the correction in front of them mortified her and she'd reluctantly gulped down two more of the dry, flat cakes while Cole stood and watched, arms across his chest. *Brute.*

The gun had been a tragic mistake, now tucked away in Cole's belt probably until such time he saw fit to give it back to Junior. She'd be an angel now, perfectly obedient. He'd have no excuse to spank her.

She wondered if he would find one. Though she feared punishment, a small part of her, a part that she kept hidden in denial, was attracted to his utter control.

As they began their journey again, the sun dipping low on the horizon, a chill crept over Aida, and she shivered.

"Cold, darlin'?" Cole asked over her shoulder. Justice was riding beside them now, and he looked sharply at Cole, a brief look that was nearly lost on Aida before he turned front again and went back to stoically ignoring her.

"I'm fine," Aida lied, another shiver betraying her.

He grunted, clearly not appeased by her answer, and growled, "You scoot up closer to me if need be. We ride on until we get to our next stop, but it shouldn't be long."

She obediently scooted closer to him, his flank pushed up against her back, his warmth seeping through her thin garments. She could feel his hardened muscles against her, and her eyes focused on his large, strong hands holding the reins. She shivered, but this time not from cold. She was helpless to control the primal attraction to his authority and power.

Cole spoke over his shoulder. "An hour's hard ride'll bring us to Saddle Creek, two before we get to Lawson's just after dark."

He dug in his spurs, and his horse picked up speed, but seconds later, he pulled the reins taut in his hand with a loud, "Whoa!" He held a hand up to the rest of his crew and they all careened to a halt. They were surrounded, a semi-circle of dark riders closing in on them. Aida inhaled deeply, moving closer to Cole as the men neared. She couldn't see their faces, but wondered if they'd been caught by the local sheriff, and if justice would be meted out. She shifted on her seat with mixed feelings. Though she longed to be free of Cole's gang, she feared the inevitable: being back under the same roof as her father. It was imperative she get to the next town. She needed to escape.

The largest, darkest of the group of men on horses

sauntered up to Cole, lifting his Stetson, his hand resting lazily on his gun. "Is that who I think it is? It ain't Cole Clemens and his crew now, is it?" His voice was low and something about his demeanor made the little hairs stand on end along Aida's arms, fear pricking along her neck. He seemed more like a man who'd get along with Justice rather than Cole or Junior. His beady little eyes zoned in on Aida, before dipping to her creamy chest and ample thighs. He nearly licked his lips.

Cole stiffened in his seat, but when he spoke, his voice was surprisingly familiar, even congenial. "If it ain't Monty and the gang," he said with a reluctant smile.

Monty spat on the ground, the thick brown stream making Aida's stomach churn. The dark rider grinned at Cole, his teeth still brown from the chewing tobacco. His face was thin and narrow, a deep scar running straight across his cheek nearly down to his chin. The thin slits of his eyes reminded Aida of a savage animal. She shivered. The other men sat upon their horses as if waiting for a cue from him.

Aida instinctively pulled even closer to Cole.

"Damn," Monty said, while a wicked grin spread over his face. "Here I was thinkin' we'd get a little fun in and shake up some travelers afore we turn in for the night. Maybe get lucky and land us a lady or two to share." He spat again on the ground. Aida felt the bile rise in her throat, but stared at him bravely.

Cole chuckled mirthlessly. Aida watched as Cole and Monty talked to each other, neither at ease, but both familiar. Cole didn't trust the dark man and it seemed the feeling was mutual.

"Ain't much help, then," Cole said with what seemed forced camaraderie. "Got me a hostage but you know I don't share my women. I'm selfish like that. Too bad we just let one go. But you keep up to Lawson's and Lawson'll sort you fine."

Justice glanced sharply at Cole, but Cole didn't meet his eyes.

Monty lifted the reins and his horse tripped a bit closer to Cole. His voice dipped low, his eyes wicked slits. "Is that right?" he said in a low growl. "Rumor has it you kidnapped a girl back in Hollow Creek. Got a sheriff no bigger'n a half-grown coon dog sniffin' every tree and bush. Seems someone's pa's got a heavy purse, and ain't stoppin' 'til he gets his little girl back. Might this be your pretty little victim?" He reached a hand out to stroke Aida's hair. She stiffened and held her breath.

"Lay off, Monty," growled Junior, and Aida could've kissed him, but Cole held up a hand.

To Aida's relief, Monty turned away from her, and his narrowed eyes fixed on the blond cowboy. Though his eyes were on Junior, he spoke to Cole. "You still let boys barely weaned off their ma's titties in your crew?" He spat again on the ground, shaking his head. Justice snorted, Junior's eyes flashed, but all men looked to Cole as Monty's men chuckled darkly. Aida's eyes flicked over them. Suddenly her captors seemed almost benign beside the men who sported soiled bandannas, chaps splattered liberally with mud, and narrowed, wicked eyes. Even their horses seemed thinner, angrier, and more savage.

"You know my crew well, Monty," Cole said in a voice as low as a rattler sneaking through the underbrush. Aida knew that deep drawl. It was the voice he used when he was angriest. Whereas others would grow louder when angry, Cole grew softer. He was dangerous at any time of day, but lethal when his voice grew soft. "You know they're like brothers."

To Aida's relief, fear tripped across Monty's features and his eyes darted to Doc, then Justice. He swallowed and his eyes softened, as if he were suddenly repentant and ready to convince Cole to leave them be. Monty forced a laugh. "I do," he said. "Oh, I do. Seems you're down a man, though?"

Cole nodded. "Preach had an errand for me. Seems you're down a man, too?"

Monty shrugged, eyes growing cold again. "One

betrayed me. Put a bullet in 'im last town over, tossed into the river." The three men beside him each spat on the ground as if on cue. Aida felt her stomach churn. "You know I don't cotton to traitors."

"A point we agree on then," Cole said, and to Aida's surprise, his defensive stance seemed to dissolve into friendliness. "Can't say that I blame you. You all stoppin' to eat? We're just takin' a break for the night. You're welcome to join us."

They were not just stopping for a break. What had gotten into him?

"Sure thing," Monty said, turning to his crew. "We break to eat. Ain't every day we meet hospitality, boys." His eyes focused on Aida. He licked his lips. "Maybe if we're lucky, we'll even get some dessert."

CHAPTER TEN

When it is dark enough, you can see the stars. — Ralph Waldo Emerson

Damn it all to hell. Cole barely contained his fury as he got down from his horse.

Meeting up with Monty was part of the whole fucking plan, but meeting up with him before they'd even gotten to Lawson's was *not*. And why did Cole's protective ire rise when Monty focused his filthy eyes on Aida? She was nothing to him. He'd seen Monty in action, though. He'd seen him tear the dress of a woman not a month prior, the wife of a man who owed him money. He'd ruthlessly murdered the man, taken his wife as his own, then given her over to each one of his men in turn to do with as they pleased. Men the likes of Monty disgusted Cole. Though he was no angel himself, he held fast to certain principles and rued the day Monty escaped hanging.

But his plan would be shot to hell if he couldn't convince Monty they were on the same side. Fucking Monty and his lowlife crew.

He had to keep his eye on Monty, feign friendship and allegiance to the same wrong side of the law.

"You know the routine," Cole said to Doc. "Usin' up the rest of the supplies we've got now'll do us best until we can restock at Lawson's."

Doc nodded, squatting low and starting a fire to cook, as Monty and his men dismounted from their horses.

Cole bit out instructions to his men. "Justice, you water the horses and see to their food." He turned to Aida, still astride the horse and spoke low enough that only Junior and Aida could hear him. "Normally, I'd have you do the womanly tasks, but today, that'll be up to Junior."

Cole crooked a finger at Junior. Junior's brow furrowed, and he looked like he was about to protest, but before he said a word, Cole removed Junior's gun from his belt and handed it to him. Junior's eyes momentarily widened, then looked up at Cole apprehensively. Good. He knew he deserved to be punished for losing his weapon, but Cole would play his cards carefully with Monty watching. And given Monty's insulting Junior just now, Cole did not want to heap coal on Junior's already wounded pride.

"Lost my gun," Junior muttered.

"Is that right?" Cole asked sternly, fixing Junior with a look that made him squirm.

"Yes, sir," Junior said. "I'm sorry."

Cole spoke low so that no one could hear him. "Tonight you'll do cleanup, first watch, and last watch." Each men took one shift, and the bookend order would be difficult, especially when they were down a man. Junior nodded as Cole continued, his voice harsh and corrective. "And when you're on guard, you think about how it'd be if you came across Monty alone and you had no metal to save your hide. You think about what it'd be like if Monty tried to hurt one of us, or stick his filthy cock in that girl and all you had to defend yourself was your own two fists against Monty's metal." Junior closed his eyes briefly, and Cole knew he'd gotten through to him. A man in Cole's crew had to be armed, at all times, and it was a mistake deserving of punishment.

"Yes, sir," Junior repeated, taking the gun from Cole and tucking it into his holster.

"You listen to me," Cole said. Junior raised his eyes to him, and Cole stared at him. Junior was prepared to take the rest of the lecture like a man. Good. But Cole was done lecturing. "I heard what Monty said. We all did. He'll pay for that, you mark me," he whispered. "You know how I run this crew. And I ain't never takin' no boy who ain't worth his salt. You got that? We'd have been strung up from the highest rafters in Carson if you hadn't been with us last month, and I well know it."

Junior's eyes softened, and he nodded. "Then why're we with them? Eatin' dinner? Makin' friends?"

"You'll see," Cole said, straightening. He'd only tell Junior as much as he needed to know. He'd only tell *any* of them as much as they needed to know. "For now, you do as you're told. Go help Doc."

Junior obediently went over to Doc. Cole reached his hands to Aida's waist and helped her down. He could tell from the look on her face she'd heard all, but she kept her tongue. As her feet hit the ground, he drew her to him in a quick embrace, and this time it was not for show, but instinctive. She did not stiffen but gave into it. "That's a good girl," he whispered in her ear. "You stay away from this crew. You stay near me. So help me, Aida, I don't want you out of my sight. You hear me?"

She nodded briefly before she pulled away.

Monty would burn in hell for what he'd done. But if Cole had his way, he'd pay long before then.

• • • • • • •

"Tell me there's more than beans and *cornbread*," Aida mumbled, her lips pursed.

She'd endured the raucous meal, as Monty and his gang regaled Cole's crew with tales of their most recent exploits. Aida was no doubt horrified by their deplorable manners.

Cole couldn't help being rarely sickened himself. God almighty, who ate with one side of his mouth and chewed tobacco with the other? Disgusting.

He was so intent on keeping an eye on Monty and his men that he'd nearly forgotten Aida was there. She'd sat quietly by his side, but as he glanced at her now, he noted the flash of her eyes, the thinned lips, her arms tucked tight against her chest. And damn, if she got any closer to him she'd be sitting in his lap.

Still, she couldn't be allowed to carry on with such comments. Cole fixed her with a stern look. "Beans and cornbread fill our bellies," he said in a low voice, so that he wouldn't be overheard. "And you'll eat what you're given without griping."

She scoffed, tossing her head. "Where I'm from, we eat a varied diet," she said, her teeth gritted.

What the hell was she playing at? Did the girl *want* her backside blistered? He reached for her chin and drew her face to his, tilting her head up, his fingers grasping firmly enough she winced.

He leaned in so he could whisper in her ear, "Where *I* come from, little girls do as they're told unless they want to be taken across their daddy's lap."

She yanked her chin away from him and looked away. Shit. She was pulling this *now*? He scraped the last of his food with his spoon and ate it quickly, before he stood and handed his bowl and Aida's to Doc. He took her by the hand and squeezed, pulling her so that she stood close by his side.

Her lips were still pursed, and she continued muttering. "Crick in my neck the size of a goose egg. Filthy men who eat with their mouths open. My dress needs a good scrub, and this coffee is the worst swill I've ever downed in my life." She tried fruitlessly to pull her hand away from his, but he held fast. He'd not abide brats at any time, least of all at a time when her safety was in a precarious position. Cole held tight to her hand and clenched his jaw.

"Aida, you mind your tongue," he ordered.

To his surprise, she finally yanked her hand away from him, planted both hands on her hips, and glared. "*No.*"

A sudden flash of shock hit him a split second before his instincts kicked in. Didn't matter what had gotten into the little brat. Didn't matter who was there, or that they had a schedule to keep. She needed a firm hand. She needed a good, hard spanking to get her head on straight. His gaze flitted to his strap before he turned his head, narrowing his eyes on the thin branches of a nearby birch. The strap would be loud and draw unwanted attention. He needed something that would be quiet and sting enough to make a good, lasting impression.

Doc eyed him wordlessly as he stacked the dirty bowls. Cole tucked Aida by his side, and marched her past the rest of the men. Junior stood with his arms crossed, his eyes focused on Monty in undisguised hatred. At least they'd be able to get by him without raising his goddamn protective instincts of all things feminine. Justice sat close enough to Monty's crew that one would think he was one of them, laughing his fool head off at something one of Monty's men was saying to him. The sight set Cole's nerves on edge. It might do well to feign friendship, but he wondered how much Justice was actually feigning. He was not amused by the fact that her behavior was taking him away from what he needed to do here, with his men. She'd get another good round for that.

"Let go of my hand," Aida hissed.

He held her hand harder. "One more word, little girl," he warned. "One more word and I'll bare your backside in front of all of them."

He regretted the words the second they left his mouth, as Cole never made idle threats. But he'd spoken too soon. He didn't want to bare her in front of the other men, but now that he'd said it, he *would* follow through, if only because he was a man of his word. Better to teach her he meant what he said than risk her losing the edge of fear she'd been taught in the short time they'd been together. But fortunately, the threat had the desired effect, and she fell into silent but furious step beside him.

"We'll be back soon," he muttered to Doc, who merely nodded and continued scraping the dishes clean. Cole felt the eyes of Monty and his crew on his back, but he continued dragging her along with him down to a secluded area, wooded but dimly lit with moonlight.

"You're hurting my hand," she protested, trying again to pull away.

"Darlin', I'm gonna hurt more than your hand."

"You brute!" she said in a furious whisper.

"At your service," he replied with a dark chuckle. "And you're a brat, so don't we make a pair."

"Let *go*!" she said, trying again to pull away, and she even kicked her foot at him. They were now a good enough distance away from the rest of the crew, so he no longer had to endure her childish fits in silence. He spun her around and gave her two rapid swats over her clothed bottom, which made her stomp the ground, but he held fast. Dragging her to a tall white birch tree, he pushed her so that her back was up against it. Her eyes flashed at him, splotches of angry red on her cheeks as she glared.

His own anger rose as he narrowed his eyes at her. "Young lady, you've earned yourself a good lickin'. You'll stand here until I call you to me, and if you move, I'll finish our little talk tonight with a good round with my strap." He paused and dropped his voice. "If you think I'm lyin', darlin', try me."

Though she still glared at him, she stayed put as he drew a knife from his belt and cut a good-sized switch from the birch, thin and supple, long enough to leave a lasting impression when he took her over his knee. He remembered from his boyhood the schoolmaster's fondness for the birch; the sting that would last for hours after a switching. It would do well. He quickly stripped and prepared the switch, lashing it through the air against his palm to test it. Satisfied that it packed a good sting, he beckoned to Aida.

"Come here," he growled. That she'd taken him away from keeping his eye on Monty was no small infraction. He'd get to the bottom of why she'd been so defiant after he blistered her backside.

Still holding her chin erect, she marched over to him angrily, stomping on the leaves and twigs until she stood in front of him. Again, he wondered if her defiance was intentional. She knew he wouldn't abide such behavior, and now that her spanking was imminent, she stared him down fearlessly. Did she *need* him to spank her? Did a small part of her have to challenge him?

When she reached him, he grasped her elbow and glanced around him. A large stump was a few feet away, next to a fallen tree trunk. The stump would do well. He dragged her over and sat down. It was an easy matter to draw her straight across both knees.

As her warm belly pressed up against his lap, his cock hardened, and he nearly groaned out loud. Damn her curvy, inviting figure. He remembered the fevered pitch of her moans as he'd made her climax. The sudden vision of her luscious form, naked, beneath him on the clean white sheets in a room at Lawson's, almost made him lose his focus. Sweet Jesus, what would it be like to have those tantalizing moans under him as he ground into her? Her soft, gentle curves beneath his hardened muscles as he mounted her?

But no. He could not dwell on anything but the matter at hand, and there was a naughty little girl who needed a good, hard spanking.

Placing the switch down beside him, he lifted her skirts quickly. His hands itched to stroke her, his mouth to take her. He wanted to ravish her until she groaned in ecstasy at his mercy. She wiggled in protest when his hand went to her drawers to pull them down, writhing to get away, but he held fast.

Her voice took on a different tone, no longer hard and

defiant but now pleading. "Oh, please, Cole. Not on the bare skin! Not with a switch!"

There was something endearing about hearing his name in her lovely voice, but he'd still not be dissuaded. "Do I want to hear you call me Cole?"

Her shoulders slumped, and she shook her head from side to side. "No, Daddy."

"Good girl. You're hardly in a position to be tellin' me what to do, little girl," he said, as he pulled her drawers straight down to her ankles. Her hand shot out to block him but he pinned it quickly. She moaned, likely more so from apprehension and fear than anything, but the mere sound had him shifting with arousal. When she was sufficiently vulnerable, the smooth skin of her backside bare, he lifted the switch and touched her bottom with it.

"You were a naughty little girl just now, Aida," he chided. "And Daddy won't abide such behavior." He lifted the switch and snapped it against her bottom. She flinched and yelped, as an angry red stripe rose on her creamy white skin. The switch whistled through the air before it landed again in a quiet *thwap* against her skin. He paused several seconds between each swat.

"You'll eat what I give you."

Again the switch landed in earnest. She jumped and whimpered. He delivered three more firm swats before he spoke again.

"You'll not defy me."

Another hard lash of the switch broke her resolve, and she cried out loud.

"The men we're with now will just as soon kill you as they would look at you, taking their fill of your sweet pussy in turn. Defying me now puts you at risk."

The swish and thud of the switch fell in earnest now. Her bottom was striped in angry red welts as he continued. He wanted her to feel the sting for days. He wanted her to remember what happened to little girls who defied their daddies.

"You'll do what I say, and you'll obey me without question," he continued. "I don't care if I have to take you over my knee every damn morning when you wake up, and across my lap again before you go to bed at night."

Thwap. The switch cut across her thighs, eliciting a scream of pain, before he lashed across her thighs again. She twisted her torso, trying to get away from the pain, but he held fast. He stopped his lecture, letting the punishing cut of the switch do the talking.

Her howls of protest quieted as Cole continued the switching. Her back no longer stiffened over his lap, and she went limp, though her hands clung tenaciously to his pant leg. He paused, placing one hand on her warmed backside, rubbing her skin. "Have I made my point, young lady?"

She sniffled. "Yes." she said, her voice thick with emotion. Good. He was getting somewhere, though her spanking was not finished.

He tossed the switch to the side, his large, rough hand smoothing over her backside. His cock strained for release, but he held fast to the duty he had to perform.

"Those men up there need to be watched, Aida," he said. "But because of your naughty behavior, I had to step away from them."

He raised his hand and delivered a sound smack to her punished bottom. She gasped and squirmed, but he held fast, lifting his hand before bringing it down with another loud *crack*. The touch of skin on skin marked her, made the punishment memorable and lasting. But it also made him even harder, so much so he was tempted to let her go before he was quite finished. As he lectured her, he reminded himself *why* he had to spank her so soundly, his voice deepening as his anger rose.

"Those men would hurt you." *Swat!* "And I don't mean a crack across your backside that will wear off in time. I don't mean a spanking, little girl." *Swat!* "My job is to keep you away from them. And if I'm spendin' my time tannin' your pretty little hide, my eyes are off them and *I don't like that."* Three rapid swats fell. She was crying in earnest now. He was done.

He lifted her up and held her against his chest. It felt nice holding her like this. Sick bastard that he was, he ignored the fact that he was the one who'd caused her to cry to begin with, his protective instincts rising as her hands reached for him. Her thin frame shook, racked with sobs as he held her, weeping.

He couldn't help it. He needed to soothe her. A dim part of his mind reminded him that now would be an opportune time to garner her unmitigated trust, use it to his advantage, manipulate her into going along with him. But instinct prevailed.

"Shh, darlin'," he said. "You're safe now. I know I spanked you hard, but you're safe, Aida. You'll understand soon, but for now, you'll do what Daddy says. It's my job to take care of you. We're almost where we need to go, and it'll all be clear to you soon. You'll see. If they try to hurt you—if any of them try to hurt you—I'll kill them." The words tumbled out of his mouth before he could stop them, as he kissed her dampened cheek and smoothed a rough hand over her soft blond curls, pressing her head against his chest. He wanted nothing more than to calm her tears and still her shaking. He held her silently, rocking her against his chest.

He heard the telltale sound of a twig snapping. His head bolted up, his keen eyes taking in the forest around them. But he saw nothing.

"What is it?" she whispered, her eyes looking into his, wide and trusting, vulnerable. Without another thought, he kissed her.

God almighty, he hoped it was just a creature, and not one of the men. If Monty or his crew caught wind of anything, his plan would be shot to hell.

CHAPTER ELEVEN

Sometimes I'm terrified of my heart; of its constant hunger... the way it stops and starts. — Edgar Allan Poe

Aida wanted to protest. She wanted to push him away. But when Cole's head dipped down and his mouth found hers, though her mind said *no*, her body said *yes*.

Yes. Please. More.

It was wrong, all of it, so very wrong. He'd whipped her mercilessly. He was an outlaw. *He'd stolen her.* But never had she been attracted to a man like Cole. The men she'd met as of late, the rich dandies who called on her at home, were nothing like her captor. Their hands were pale and soft, their clothes impeccably clean. They smelled of clover and mint, and she stood taller than a few. Their dainty speech and perfect manners sickened her. She hated them, all of them. They all reminded her of her father.

The rough stubble of Cole's bearded face scratched her as his mouth, soft in comparison to everything else about him, met hers in unapologetic greed. He wanted her. His tongue plunged into her mouth, and arousal zinged through her core. Her body had been taut before, wound and closed and properly chastened, but now she was split open, laid bare, heat galloping through her veins and arousal across her chest as his raw, powerful hands raked over her breasts. His fingers nimbly found her nipples, squeezing with just the right amount of pressure so a low moan hummed between them as they kissed.

He pulled his mouth away and cursed, the guttural growl somehow making her need him more. Everything in her instinctively yearned for his power, his strength, his unabashed masculinity. He raked his fingers through her hair, tugging her head back with surprising tenderness, though she felt the pull on her scalp, a reminder of his unbridled strength. He made her feel small, feminine, and somehow beautiful. His whiskered mouth graced her cheek with a kiss.

"You'll be a good girl, Aida," he said, and she nodded. Yes. Yes, she would, she'd do anything he said. "You won't give Daddy reason to punish you again like that."

Daddy.

Why did hearing him say that make her thighs clench, her nipples tighten against the bodice of the dress? It was so *wrong*.

She swallowed, utterly consumed with her need for him, as she gasped a response. "No. I'm sorry." Her voice caught at the end. She *was* sorry.

She'd needed to defy him, needed to push. The feeling of being out of control was unsettling. But now as he held her close to his chest, she felt calmed. No longer out of control or angry. He was strong. He would protect her. She'd needed the stern reminder. Her entire life she'd been allowed to do as she'd wanted. She'd been spoiled terribly. Cole was the first man who had ever held her to a higher standard, and though she'd deny it, deep down inside she felt the magnetic pull of his authority. It was calming and undeniably erotic.

"I want to hold you," he said, his mouth trailing down to her neck. His tongue flicked out, licking the bare skin of her collarbone. She gasped at the sensation as his teeth gently nipped the sensitive skin at her neck. "I want to lay you down and strip you." His voice was so deep and raspy it traipsed across her skin like liquid fire. "I want to taste you," he growled. "Every bit of you. Your mouth, your breasts, and your sweet little pussy."

She closed her eyes against the flames that licked through her. God, if only…

"I whipped you now, and I don't regret it," he said. "But you took that whippin' like a good girl. And in my book, good girls get rewards." He paused before he continued. "I forget nothin', Aida." His voice hardened, but the roughness of it made her insides tremble. "I remember who deserves to be punished. I mete out punishment when the time is right." His tongue flicked out against her skin again, and her hips bucked with need. "But I also remember who deserves to be rewarded." His hand traveled beneath the layers of dress, one finger dipping between her legs. "Can you be a patient girl? Obey Daddy? Stay away from those men up there, and stay by my side?"

"Yes," she moaned. Anything. She'd do anything.

"Try again, darlin'?"

It didn't feel wrong this time. She didn't feel anger. Now, she reveled in it. "Yes, *Daddy*."

∙ ∙ ∙ ∙ ∙ ∙ ∙

Cole walked her back up to camp, and as the cool air hit him, his haze of arousal began to lift.

Goddamn it.

What had come over him just now? All he'd wanted was her obedience. He didn't have time for anything short of complete obedience from *everyone*. He wanted her to trust him, yes, and it was far easier to get it from her that way. But damn, if he hadn't been sincere back there. He didn't want Monty and his boys seeing him come back to camp with Aida, so he walked up ahead, caught Junior's attention, and flagged him over. "Take her to the creek and see she gets herself ready to sleep," he ordered. Junior was more than happy to obey. Cole ignored Aida's look of confusion and sent her on her way.

It wouldn't do to fall for the girl. He was so consumed with anger, he almost missed his brother standing up against the tree, one leg propped up as he chewed before he spat. Chewing tobacco. Cole's crew had none. Monty had plenty.

"Why'd you whip the girl again?" Justice asked. So he *had* seen.

Cole frowned. "She disobeyed me. Had a fit worthy of a spoiled brat. Trust me, she was askin' for it." How much had Justice seen? "And who told you it was okay to spy on me?"

"Wasn't spyin," Justice said with a shrug, though his eyes shifted to the side and he didn't meet Cole's gaze. "Had to take a piss, and happened to see you take a switch to her." He shrugged. "Just wondered why." He started to walk away but looked briefly at Cole. "You need to do it again, don't forget your brother," he said. "I'd be happy to save you the hassle and whip her myself."

Cole growled. The hell he would.

The men were rolling out their bedrolls, the fire mere embers now. Monty was talking in low tones to his men on the other side of camp. Doc was already lying down and likely asleep, as Junior and Aida came back up to camp. They were talking amiably, but both quieted when they approached Cole.

"Junior, watch the fire for your first watch," he said. "For the last one, you'll wake us early, before sunrise. You hear?"

Junior nodded. "Yes, sir," he said.

Cole crooked a finger at him. When Junior was close enough to hear a whisper, Cole spoke quietly. "When you watch, you keep an eye on Monty. Anything out of place, you wake me. You hear?"

Junior's eyes narrowed. "Yes, sir," he said. "I don't trust 'em."

"Good. You ought not." He clapped Junior on the shoulder and was pleased to see Junior straighten, walking with pride to his post.

Cole tossed down his bedroll and laid it out. "You ready?" he asked Aida.

Her eyes cast down shyly, she nodded. She'd stripped down to her chemise, a blanket wrapped tightly around her shoulders.

He got in first, then gestured for her to join him. Even Monty's men had turned in, and it was just the two of them now. The crackle of the dying fire was the only sound in the still evening. Cole tucked her against him, and as her sweet bottom nestled back, his cock hardened. God, he wanted her so badly. He'd have to be patient.

Still, that didn't mean she had to go without.

He slowly, carefully dipped his hands between her legs and lifted the thin chemise. She shifted back against him, her backside pressing tighter against his cock, welcoming him. He grinned against the soft curls below his chin as he stroked her, slick with arousal and ready for him. He heard her gasp. They didn't make a sound and barely moved as he embraced her, one arm going to her chest and gently kneading her breast as he stroked her between her legs. She opened her legs wider as he stroked softly but firmly, lazily circling her with his finger. He could feel her mounting as he stroked and he continued until he heard another soft gasp. He could tell she was trying with all she could to be quiet, but her body shook beneath him with the power of her climax. Her hips bucked and her head dipped down as she shoved her fist in her mouth. He glanced quickly around. No one was the wiser. When she stilled, he removed his hand from between her legs and tucked it around her slim waist, lowering his mouth to her ear.

"That's a good girl," he whispered. "Sleep now, darlin'."

She was silent, but she nestled her bottom up against him. Soon he heard her soft, steady breathing.

He wasn't falling for her. No. This would earn her trust,

and that had to happen. She might hate him when all was done, but until then, he'd do what he could to protect her.

● ● ● ● ● ● ● ●

They'd risen before the sun, eating nothing but hardtack with strong coffee as Aida sat next to Cole, wordlessly downing the acrid brew and dry food. She felt as humble and meek as she'd been since she met him, though she hated herself for the way she'd allowed him to have his way with her.

As they rode hard all day long, her backside still stung from the switching and she wondered if she found a looking glass in town if she'd have welts or bruises. She dipped her head down shyly when she remembered being stripped and taken across Cole's knee. She looked discreetly to the side, taking him in. Dark, hardened, muscled, his jaw clenched sternly as he eyed Monty's crew when he tipped his head to the side. Her hands tightened around his large hands, and she couldn't help the feelings that rose in her. The jostling of the horse, memory of the whipping, vivid recollection of Cole's hands between her legs bringing her to ecstasy… it was all too much. She could not hate him. And despite every logical lecture she gave herself, it simply didn't work. She wanted him. What would happen when they reached their destination? The desire to run no longer held the same appeal.

When they took a small break to eat and water the horses, and Monty came to talk to him, Cole stepped between Aida and Monty. It was a move she could only assume was meant to protect her. *Was* it? Was he truly trying to protect her?

They talked in low voices, and Aida wished she could hear them. She didn't like not knowing what the cruel-looking man with the scar across his face had planned. Her instincts told her that if Cole and his men weren't there, Monty would do evil, wicked things to her, far worse than

Cole ever had.

As they spoke, Monty turned to her, raking his eyes across her chest, leering. He swallowed and licked his lips. Cole didn't move, but Aida could feel him tense before Monty turned and walked away.

"Come with me," Cole ordered, dragging her with him. He turned and spoke over his shoulder to Doc. "Takin' the girl to the privy," he said. "She'll get freshened up. When I get back I expect camp broken down and you three ready to ride."

Junior tipped his hat, Justice nodded, and Doc saluted. Why did her heart stutter at the way he ruled—calm and steady, with a firm hand? There was kindness in this man, even though it lay buried. She'd heard the way he'd praised Junior after meting out consequences. And hadn't he held her after he'd whipped her? But no. No, that was all for show. He hadn't really meant it.

She kept her eyes cast down as they walked to the creek. She wanted to berate herself for the feelings she could not tamp down. Her body and mind would not obey logic or reason. She felt riddled with a sudden desire to cry.

"You move quickly, Aida," Cole said, taking her hand in his and marching her along swiftly. "How's that backside feelin'?"

She raised her head sharply to look at him. "Sore," she said.

He pursed his lips. "Good. You gonna behave yourself?"

"Of course," she said with a toss of her head.

He slowed, and his voice dipped down. "Try that again, darlin'."

Aida inhaled, then exhaled slowly. She didn't want to call him Daddy again.

It troubled her how much she liked it.

But she also didn't want to land herself over his lap again, either.

"Yes, Daddy," she said. "I'll be a little angel."

His eyes warmed at that, and he tugged her a bit closer.

"That's a good girl," he said. "I like hearing you say that."

"Which part?" she asked before she thought, her mouth getting ahead of her. "The part about being an angel, or when I call you Daddy?"

They walked in silence toward the creek, and he didn't respond at first. In the quiet that lay between them for several seconds, Aida regretted her question. But when he spoke, his voice was surprisingly gentle. Sincere, even.

"Daddy. I like hearing you call me Daddy."

Now that he was actually speaking to her rather than ordering her or chastising her, she couldn't help but push further. "Why?"

His jaw clenched. "Because I'm a sick bastard, sweetheart."

No. No, he wasn't. Yes, he'd whipped her. He'd taken her. But she couldn't believe it, no matter how hard she tried. She simply couldn't believe this man was evil. And though part of her wanted to stop her mind from behaving with such naïveté, she felt there could be honesty between them. What did she have to lose?

"You're not," she said. "I know you're not. You're more like me than you care to admit."

He scoffed at that as they reached the creek's edge, and when he turned to her, his eyes had hardened. "I'm a spoiled little princess?" he leered.

A lump rose in her throat and she yanked her hand away from him. Maybe he wasn't good deep down after all. Maybe he *was* a sick bastard. She wouldn't look at him.

No, she wanted to say. *Not spoiled.*

Angry. Hurt. Guarded.

Like me.

But what difference did it make anyway? She was already tainted, damaged goods, her innocence having been stripped from her long ago and no one would ever love her the way she longed to be loved.

She would not bridge the gap between them. She'd obey him to avoid being whipped again, and plan her escape.

• • • • • • •

The minute the words left his mouth, Cole wanted to kick himself. They'd come so far, and she'd finally begun to trust him, and when she let her guard down for a minute, he'd slammed the door on her. Her eyes had shuttered. Her hand had pulled away from him, and he'd let her.

This was only about regressing to where they'd been, and he'd have to get her back in his good graces. At least he told himself that. Then why did he feel a deep pang of regret in his gut? Why did he want to pull her close to him and apologize? Why did he want to kiss her, and see her eyes trusting and open again?

He waited in stony silence while she freshened by the creek, then he took her back to camp. Right before they reached the others, he pulled her close to him. He had to make her feel a little better.

"Anything could happen in the next town, Aida. You stay by my side and do as you're told." She pulled her chin away but he yanked her face back to his with one swift move. "You know what'll happen."

Her chin lifted proudly, she looked him square in the eye. "I do. I won't disobey you." But she was hurt. He could see it in the way she pulled back from him and wouldn't hold his gaze. "No need to worry, *Daddy*. I'll do what you say."

The barb stung more than he cared to admit.

Damn it all to hell. Didn't matter if she was hurt. What did he care if she was upset by his crass words? She *was* a spoiled little princess. If she wasn't, he wouldn't have had to take her across his lap to spank the brat out of her. He turned from her, yanking her hand so that she had to trot to keep up with him. When they got back to others, no one was ready yet.

"I told you to be done when I got back here," he growled at Junior, who was still tying up the bedrolls.

"Yes, sir," Junior said, looking at Cole curiously as he stormed past.

"You ready to ride?" Cole said sharply to Justice, who merely lifted his brows and nodded in silence. "I said be ready when we got back," Cole spit out. Justice glared in return.

Cole lifted Aida up on the saddle, before he swung up behind her. "Let's go, boys."

He dug his spurs into his horse's flanks and took off at a gallop. The others could catch up.

• • • • • • •

They circled the nondescript town as night fell, each pulling their horses up to Cole's lead in silence. Aida watched everything, taking in each detail. She tried to piece together what she'd learned. Lawson's was a stop along the way, but a crucial one. Monty rode up to Cole, and though he whispered, Aida heard every word.

"Sheriff's likely three sheets to the wind by now," Monty said in Cole's ear. "Once he's down, the rest is child's play."

"Of course," Cole said. "I know." Aida knew by now their identities could be revealed at any moment. All it would take would be one person noticing Monty's scar, or Cole's dark eyes from a 'Wanted' poster, and their plans would be shot. If only she could get far enough from Cole to get to someone… but as the wheels turned, Monty's eyes focused on her.

Monty looked at Aida's hands around Cole's waist. "You're sweet on her, aren't you?" he asked Cole with undisguised contempt. Aida felt her heart flutter. Sweet on her. Cole wasn't sweet on her. He hated her. Hated that she was spoiled and wealthy. He wouldn't have whipped her, taken her from her home, and spoken with such contempt for her if he didn't find her repulsive.

"Course not," Cole bit out. "I told you she's my captive. I need her close so she doesn't give us away." Even though

Aida expected as much, her belly twisted. It still hurt to hear it.

"Yeah, I heard you," Monty continued. "And I well know there's likely a pretty price on her head in Litchfield," he said, as he spat a stream of brown on the ground. "So you're carryin' her to earn that prize, but you're fallin' for her."

"Fuck you," Cole hissed and Monty's face spread into a leer.

"No, Cole," Monty whispered. He spurred his horse to walk within inches of Cole. "Fuck her. You know who I am. We meet up with Pearson soon. And you know Pearson makes me look like a saint. You fuck her, or Pearson'll be haulin' her by the hair to his own fucking chambers."

Cole looked sharply at Monty. "Pearson?"

Monty merely pursed his lips and nodded. Aida's heart stuttered so that she could hardly think, see, or even feel, as Monty pulled ahead of Cole. "I'd just as soon shoot her as look at her," he said. "But if you let our plans go to hell because Pearson can't keep his cock in his pants, I'll kill you." Monty's eyes raked over Aida, and she pulled closer to Cole as Monty trotted away.

Cole swore vehemently, before turning to her. "Whatever happens next," he said in a low growl. "Whatever happens next, you do whatever you can to trust me. I was a bastard earlier by the creek, but I'm tellin' you now, Aida, it'll get worse tonight. Just listen to what I tell you."

Aida felt frozen in place, both Monty's and Cole's words filling her with fright.

Fuck her.

Her heart thundered in her chest as they stealthily trotted their horses up to a back door of a saloon. When they arrived, the door swung open, and an older man with graying hair and shrewd, calculating eyes gestured for them to come in.

"Let my men water your horses," the man said, "and

come on in."

Cole swung down from his horse, then lifted Aida, as the man's eyes went to him.

"Cole, you've got yourself a girl?" the man asked with surprise. Aida wondered why he was surprised. Was it because Cole wasn't the type to have a girl? Or that he'd take her traveling with him? In any event, her sense of foreboding increased, and her heart twisted at Cole's words.

"Not my girl," Cole said. "Can't talk about it, Lawson. That said, tonight, no ladies for me. I need rest, and the girl will warm my bed."

Lawson nodded and gestured for them to come in. Each quietly dismounted, Junior and Justice seeing to the horses with Lawson's men as Cole traipsed into Lawson's back door. Cole stiffened when he entered the room, and to Aida's surprise, he put a protective hand on her arm. His eyes had darkened, his jaw clenched.

At the table sat a tall, lanky man. His hair was a nondescript brown, his eyes muddy and unfocused. He had several empty shot glasses on the table. Aida felt as if she were a specimen on display when the man's eyes roved over her.

"Pearson," Cole said with a nod.

The man called Pearson looked from Cole, to Aida, to Monty, then over each member of both Monty's and Cole's crews that had come in.

"Pleasure, as always," he said, his voice low and hard. He got to his feet, his eyes filled with contempt as he glared at Cole. Aida felt the air shift in the room as the man turned to Lawson. "You got the rooms upstairs cleared out?"

Lawson nodded vigorously. "Oh, yes, sir," he said.

"Good," Pearson said and he trudged with heavy boots on the wooden floor, creaking to where a small staircase to the far right almost lay hidden. "Upstairs," Pearson growled.

Aida felt Cole tug her along almost fiercely, his hand hurting hers, fingers crushed against the tenacious grip.

"You're hurting me," she whispered. Cole did not reply,

simply following Monty and Pearson up the rickety stairs in stone-faced silence, though his grip lessened a bit.

When they reached the top of the stairs, Aida could see a hallway with several rooms. Cole gestured for Junior, Justice, and Doc to take a few rooms, while Monty's men clambered into rooms of their own, until only Pearson, Cole, and Aida remained in the hall. Pearson turned to Aida.

"So pretty," he said. "You'll give me a turn, Cole." It didn't seem like a suggestion. Aida held her breath.

Cole chuckled mirthlessly. "You know I don't share, Pearson," he said.

The man's lips turned down and he gave Cole a calculating look. "You still playing hero?"

Cole's lips thinned as he glared back at Pearson. "You know why I'm here," he said.

Pearson nodded quickly before giving Aida one more appraising look. "We'll see about that," was all he said, but as the sound of his retreating footsteps faded, Cole's arm went to her waist. Aida's thundering heart slowed just a little. The mere thought of this man touching her sent sickening shivers of dread through her. He seemed capable of anything. With a tug on her hand, Cole pulled her into the room and slammed the door.

CHAPTER TWELVE

Love is merely a madness; and I tell you, deserves as well a dark house and whip as madmen do. — *William Shakespeare*

Cole paced the room as Aida used the attached privy, freshening up. Her shoes were lined up next to the door and for some reason, the little shoes played at his sympathies. Aida was so young, so trusting... and could be so easily hurt. If Pearson ever got his filthy hands on her, he'd have to kill him.

The night was dark, the moon casting little light on the ground. Cole peered out the window, plotting what he would do next. If Pearson and Monty thought for a minute that Cole wasn't who he said he was... Pearson already doubted him, had doubted him since a month earlier when Cole had refused to shoot an innocent woman in a raid at a bank. Pearson never dirtied his hand with the raids, but when word came to him that Cole hadn't pulled the trigger, Cole knew then a seed of doubt had been planted. He had to work this perfectly, and if he did, Pearson's presence here and now could aid his ultimate plan well. Very well. But it was a razor's edge he walked until then.

A sharp knock came on the door to the room. Stalking

over, Cole yanked the door open. Junior stood, staring at him with wide open eyes. Cole gestured for him to come in.

Junior fidgeted nervously as Cole shut the door.

"Heard Pearson," Junior said. "Didn't know I was there. I went to go check on the horses before dinner, and Pearson was in the stable with Monty." He swallowed. Cole frowned, crossing his arms on his chest, but he gave Junior an encouraging nod.

Junior continued. "I heard Monty say you shared a bedroll overnight, and he thought you were fixin' to make her yours. Pearson said if you showed yourself weak with a woman, you couldn't be trusted, with what they have planned."

Cole's frown deepened. "Is that all?" he asked.

Junior nodded. "For now, yeah," he said. "I just thought you ought to know." Junior spoke in a low voice, with a subtle gesture that might've looked like he was swatting a fly, or flicking a speck of dust. But Cole understood, his eyes trained on the dark wooden dresser that stood between the rooms. Cole knew the implication, moving his eyes intentionally out the window so he wasn't staring at the dresser. There was a peephole between the dark wooden dresser and the bed.

Cole clapped Junior on the shoulder. "Thanks for that," he said, and Junior took his leave.

The door opened and Aida emerged. Her face had been scrubbed, her hair tidied, and her dress smoothed out. She still needed fresh clothing and a bath, but she was pretty as a picture as she was. Her eyes met his and for a moment unveiled, but when he reached for her hand, it was as if she remembered he was not to be trusted, and her eyes shuttered again.

"Come here," Cole said, tugging her hand so that she was as close to him as she'd ever been, while purposely keeping them angled away from the peephole. "You listen to me, and you listen well. No matter what happens over the next few hours, you try to understand. Remember?

Trust me, darlin'. Can you trust me?"

She glared at him, her jaw clenched.

"Trust you?" she asked helplessly. "Trust the man that took me from my home. Trust the man who whipped me over his knee. Trust the man who's holding me hostage and planning to do who-knows-what to me?" Her face frowned in disgust. "I don't trust you."

Of course she didn't. God, he'd been such a fool. He had her, right there in the palm of his hand, and now she'd turned from him again.

Spurred on by the need to make her understand what these men were capable of, he whispered in her ear, "You heard Monty talking earlier. You know what has to happen now. I promise I'll make it good for you, darlin'. But you need to do exactly what I say." He needed her to cooperate. She had to. "Do you have any idea what those men are capable of?"

Her eyes flashed. "Something worse than taking me against my will, whipping me, and holding me hostage?"

Cole chuckled darkly. "Oh, honey. That would only be them getting off to a good start. What I've seen those men do would make your toes curl."

She turned her chin away from him defiantly.

Quickly, he tugged her closer. Fear raced through her eyes as if she feared punishment, as with her last act of defiance.

"No, I'm not spankin' you right now, little girl," he said. "Though if you keep it up, you will earn a trip over Daddy's knee. No, it seems you're still angry over what I said earlier." He pulled her head down to his ear. "Darlin', it's nighttime. I still owe you a reward. And I'll give it to you." His voice dipped low as he whispered in her ear. "But they're watchin'." They could see but they could hear nothing but low murmurs, so he would have to use that to his advantage.

She started and whispered back, "Who's watching?"

He took a deep breath and exhaled, whispering, "Pearson. The guy that brought us to this room."

Her eyes widened, as he pulled her head down and crushed her mouth with his. He pushed her over to the bed, and gently but firmly made her lay back on the bed as he straddled her. Her breath came in gasps as her eyes widened, but she did not protest. She gasped, but his hand went to her mouth and he hushed her, speaking in a low whisper in her ear that couldn't be heard by anyone but her. "I'm gonna take you, Aida. Take you while they watch. But I want you to fight me. You need to struggle. Struggle, girl. It's for your own good," he said.

She shook her head from side to side, her eyes wide and frightened, and he guessed anyone who was peering in at a distance would think that she was resisting him. But he knew she wasn't shaking her head to feign resistance, but saying that she wouldn't cooperate. She was defying him.

"Aida," he warned, but she continued to glare and shake her head. Lifting his hand, he brought it down with a sharp crack to her thigh. She squealed, and he spanked her again.

"Struggle," he hissed in her ear.

Her eyes narrowed and she froze in place, not moving. She didn't believe him. Did she think he was lying?

So that was how it would be, then.

He took both of her hands and pinned them by her sides as his lips found hers. She moaned beneath him, her tongue meeting his as he took her mouth hard. She pushed her hands against him but could hardly move while he straddled her. It was an easy matter to overpower her. She wiggled helplessly beneath him, but it wasn't real enough yet, it wasn't desperate. The struggle had to be real and convincing.

He rolled off of her, sat on the bed, and hauled her straight over his lap. She squealed as he yanked her skirts up and her drawers down.

"No!" she screamed.

Now they were getting somewhere.

She flailed an arm helplessly back, her hand trying to slap his away, but he deftly pinned her hand to her lower back and slapped her naked backside, not pausing to even catch his breath as blow after blow fell. It would show those who watched him that he was in charge, in control, and that she was his captive.

He knew he was being a brute, but he also knew that playing the part of brute would be most convincing.

Yanking a fistful of her hair up, he pulled her head up.

"You gonna do what Daddy says now?" he growled, releasing her hand. She tried to get up, but he kept her in position with a hand on her lower back.

"Go to hell," she hissed, her skirts falling as she twisted herself on his lap, layers of dress and petticoats getting in his way.

The clothes would have to go.

He pushed her off his lap, standing her in front of him. Spinning her around, he quickly leaned down and removed a dagger from his boot.

"Don't move," he hissed. "You move, and you'll get hurt. *Fucking* hell, girl," he muttered under his breath. "You'll do as you're told. It's for your own good, to prove you're my captive. They can't think I have feelings for you."

He had to move quickly before she realized what he was doing. Dipping the tip of the dagger at the laced bodice in the back, he drew it down with one firm tug, expertly avoiding her sensitive skin and effectively slashing her dress clean down the center. He was prepared for her gasp and braced for her to jerk or spin around, but fortunately she chose this time to obey. Holding his dagger in his right hand, with his left he pushed her dress over her shoulders, tearing the clothes off of her until she stood in front of him stripped and naked, her undergarments pooled at her feet. She crossed her arms on her chest, glaring at him, her cheeks aflame with anger. He wanted to pull her close to him and cover her, the thought of Pearson seeing her like this infuriating. But he had to make it look real, had to show them what he was capable of.

"Don't move, Aida," he hissed. She reared back and

slapped him as hard as she could, straight across his face. He could feel the snap in his jaw and the flare of pain, which he quickly shook off.

Grasping her quickly around the waist, he hauled her over to him as he got to his feet. Pushing her to the bed belly down, she was now lying over the edge. She gasped at the sound of his buckle clasp. In a matter of seconds, his belt whizzed through the loops on his trousers. His cock was already rock hard, and spanking her would make him even harder. He doubled over his belt, holding her in place on the bed with his hand on her back. Quickly, he delivered a hard lash. She yelped and protested, but he easily overpowered her as before, lifting the belt again and administering another searing swat.

She yelled, squirming underneath him, but he ignored her, the heady excitement of overpowering her intermingling with the need to prove himself to Pearson by making her fight him. Another hard lash fell, then another, her bottom now a deep cherry red as the sound of leather hitting her bare skin resounded in the small room.

After a dozen searing lashes, he threw his belt on the floor. He wanted to hold her. He wanted to kiss her, and rock her, and call her Daddy's little girl. He wanted to turn her over, bury his face in her sweet pussy until she grasped his hair and screamed in ecstasy. But no. No, she had to submit to him or all would be lost.

She was momentarily without fight on the bed, having been stripped and spanked, so he took the opportunity to quickly unfasten his trousers. He leaned in and whispered in her right ear, the opposite from where the others could see.

"Fight me, honey," he said. "Fight me, but I'm not gonna hurt you now. I'll go slow enough so you feel me and if you focus on me, focus on submitting, it will be easier on you. You don't like it, and you won't admit it, but you're wet as hell after I've whipped you, and it'll help." She was silent, lying still beneath him. She had to fight. Grasping her hair, he tugged her head back. "*Fight me*," he ordered, with a resounding slap to the side of her thigh. She howled, twisting beneath him, as he pushed her on the bed and lifted her torso up so she was on her knees, chest down, ass in the air. God, she was beautiful.

Straddling her from behind, he nudged his cock into her pussy. "I'm gonna take you darlin'," he said. Though her eyes were closed tightly, she nodded once, just enough that he alone could see.

He wanted to go slow. He wanted to make her pleasure his goal. He grabbed a fistful of her hair and pulled hard. She gasped as he plunged his cock into her core. She tightened around him as he filled her, and he groaned out loud with the feeling. He planted his hands on her hips, driving himself hard within her. Her pussy tightened around his cock with every thrust, slick arousal welcoming him to drive deeper, push harder. Her face tipped to the side and she groaned, a primal beg for more.

He focused on her beneath him, and shoved his right hand between her body and the blanket, grasping her breast. He glared, lips pursed, eyes narrowed, hoping that it would look like he was simply ravaging her, as the fingers that were hidden from the peephole flicked and primed her nipple, desperately hoping he'd arouse her. He slowed, leaning down to her, and whispered into her ear, "Such a good girl. You're so wet for Daddy. Come for me, darlin'."

She moaned again, her eyes closed now. He flicked a tongue out to her neck and licked the sweet skin. She was panting now as he dipped a finger to her nub and stroked. Her breath hitched, and she pushed back against him with a cry, her pussy milking his cock. She finally gave in to her own release, moaning aloud as she climaxed beneath him, his own cries of pleasure mingling with hers.

She sniffled quietly. Fucking hell, he hoped the bastards who watched were gone now. They'd gotten their show. How could he take care of her now without them noticing? He slumped against her, feigning exhaustion, as he withdrew himself.

"Stay there," he hissed, pointing a finger at her so that anyone watching would think he was growling out an order. "Daddy's gonna take care of you, but you stay there."

He zipped up his trousers and made his way over to the dresser. He feigned a yawn, stretching his arms up over his head, and flicked the lantern off so they were plunged into darkness. He unbuttoned his shirt, turned to the bed, and tossed his shirt over his shoulder. He didn't look at first where it landed, but when he met her on the bed, a stream of moonlight illuminated the room. He could see how his shirt had landed in a perfect balled-up mess right on the dresser, effectively blocking the peephole. If they hadn't moved on yet, and they likely had as there were more shows to watch in the other rooms, between the light being off and the clothes on the dresser, they wouldn't see a damn thing more.

"Darlin'," he said, as he walked over to the bed, stroking a hand against her hair. "C'mere." He climbed onto the bed wearing nothing but his trousers. She turned away from him, her back to him, and pulled her legs up to her chest, a sight that made his heart twist in his chest. Did she want to protect herself from him? He closed his eyes and sat up on the bed, reaching a hand out and gently touching her back. "C'mere, baby," he whispered, but still she did not move. Another pause. "Come to your daddy now, darlin'," he said, and it was then that she finally turned to him, put her head on his chest, and cried.

• • • • • • •

Aida could see the self-loathing in his eyes. She knew he felt he'd had no choice but to do what he did. It had been an easy matter to fight him, as it wasn't just him she fought, but her own dark inclinations and instincts. For as her mind told her to turn away from him to protect herself, his strength and power was the enigmatic pull she could not resist. Her backside throbbed from the strokes of his belt, and she felt the ache in her pussy from his brutal claiming. She wanted to push him away and hate him. She *tried*.

"Leave me alone, you savage," she said, a tremor in her voice, and yet she didn't move.

"Hush, darlin'," he whispered. "If they thought I felt anything for you, they wouldn't believe I was with them," he explained. "You'll understand soon, but you had to fight me."

It made no sense. The tears were rent out of her, and she wished she could pin her hatred on him, but she couldn't. The loss of control while over his knee, or beneath him on the bed while he claimed her, made her feel more alive than she had in years, perhaps ever. She tried so hard to shove her base desires away, to tell herself not to trust him, to try to fear him. But she could not. Frustration welled in her and tears coursed down her face as he held her, strong arms holding her close to him, his bare chest under her cheek. Closing her eyes, she allowed herself a moment of wishing that somehow this was real, that somehow he meant the gentle caress.

How could she explain that the tears that fell were born from a desperate need to know he really cared for her? There was too much to dwell on. "You make me call you Daddy," she said in a half-drowsy state. "You want me to hate you."

He closed his eyes and stroked her hair, his hand on her neck drawing her closer, tighter, and yet she wanted him to hold her even *closer* and *tighter*.

"You have to hate me," he said, his voice catching at the end. "A man like me isn't good for a girl like you."

He was wrong, so very wrong.

"If you say so," she murmured. Leaning in closer to his bare chest, she kissed him gently, then her tears flowed even harder as the words flowed. She could not hate him. "You did that because you had to."

I felt like a real woman. You make me feel like a real woman.

How could she get him to see? This was the moment,

here, in the dark, when they were alone and bared to one another, when she could entrust herself to him. In the light of day, they'd have to pull up their facade again, feign hatred and maybe even violence. Who knew what tomorrow would bring?

Resting her hand flat on his chest, she spoke frankly, softly. "You were not the one who took my innocence. You were not the one who stole my purity. I was defiled long before you ever touched me."

She'd said too much.

Trust me, he'd said. Could she trust him?

"I don't hate the man I call Daddy," she whispered, tracing a finger along the prickly dark hairs on his chest. "You're the only man I've ever called that." She made a face of disgust, as if she'd eaten something rancid, and her mouth twisted. "But my father... I hate him. I hate him so much."

Cole's hand reached for the back of her neck and squeezed. "He violated you," he said, the barest lilt at the end of his voice, a question. One tilt of her head with closed eyes was all she could muster.

It still came to her in the night, the sickening hopelessness and terror, the nausea she felt when touched by soft, greedy hands. She needed the strong, sometimes painful touch of the hardened man who now held her, the loss of control with him that somehow freed her from the shackles of shame and bitter memories.

She nodded her head again. Had she said too much? But no. His grip tightened and to her surprise, his whiskered lips grazed the top of her forehead in a fierce kiss.

"Soon. So soon, you will see, it will all come to light. Until then, you need to trust me. If I say fight me, you fight me. If I say obey me, you obey me." He paused and his voice deepened. "And Aida, if I say run, you run."

A chill ran down her spine and the small hairs on her arms rose, but she nodded.

"Yes, sir," she whispered.

Cole's voice had hardened when he spoke, though he

still spoke low enough that no one would hear him but Aida. "I can't say much to you, not now. But you mark me, Aida. He'll never lay a hand on you again. His day will come. He'll pay for what he's done." His voice was deep and menacing now. "I'll see that he does."

It was with that final promise that she became devoted to him. She would trust Cole to exact justice. If anyone could, it would be him.

The tears started afresh as she squeezed her eyes shut and nodded. She hiccupped and wiped the back of her hand across her eyes. "I'm a mess," she sniffled.

"Aren't we all," he replied, which made her giggle.

"Well, I suppose we are," she said. A brief pause, then she whispered, "Daddy?"

Heat flared in his eyes. "Yes, darlin'?"

"Can they see us now?"

He shook his head. "No, honey."

"Good," she said, as she pushed herself up on her elbow and leaned in to kiss him.

CHAPTER THIRTEEN

By night, Love, tie your heart to mine, and the two together in their sleep will defeat the darkness. — Pablo Neruda

Cole held her until she was breathing softly on his chest, her body stilled and at peace. Given what would happen next, it was now imperative that she trust him. He breathed a sigh of relief, knowing that somehow, he'd broken through to her. As he watched her still, sleeping form curled up on him, he did his best to tamp down the feelings toward her that had now shifted. He'd wanted to keep her distanced, but now that they were nearing the end of their time together, he no longer wanted to push her away. She was no longer simply part of the plan. She trusted him. She submitted to him.

He'd kill the fucking bastard that violated her.

She'd still obey him, though. His jaw clenched as he thought about the dangers that lay ahead of them. He lay with her in his arms, until the wisps of moonlight gave way to dawn. Gently, he pushed her onto the bed and tucked the blanket around her as he got to his feet. He retrieved his shirt, careful to avert his eyes so he wouldn't be looking toward the peephole, buttoned it and grabbed his bandanna, tying it around his neck loosely, so he could slip it up and under his eyes when the time was right.

He checked his weapons, his dagger stuck securely in his boot and revolver in the waistband of his pants. He felt naked without his weapons on him, and now stood straighter with the cold metal against his leg and stomach.

Aida shifted in the bed, and he froze. Damn, he wished he didn't have to leave her. But the plan was more important now than ever. Junior would hate that he'd be missing the action, but he could be trusted to guard her.

Footsteps sounded in the hall, and Cole waited until he heard the low scratch at the door he'd been expecting. He undid the lock, then slowly pulled the door open until he could see the faintest stream of yellow light hit his boot, and the shadowed form of Doc waiting for him in the hall. Shutting the door behind him, he gave Doc a curt nod.

"She asleep?" Doc mouthed, pointing a finger to the room. Cole nodded, as around him other dark shadows emerged. The telltale blond tresses of Junior, Monty's swarthy cheeks and dark eyes, Justice's catlike stance and beady eyes, and several other of Monty's men Cole didn't know by name. Pearson would be hiding now, likely amidst a swarm of girls in his bed. He'd not tarnish his hands with what they were about to do, but merely funded their efforts with his own purse, taking a heavy cut.

Cole crooked a finger to Junior. Junior came to him immediately. Cole didn't want to have to tell him he'd miss the evening's raid, as it was a reward and privilege for seasoned members to take on a task so big. But before he could speak, Junior did.

"You want me to stay with the girl?" he asked.

Cole nodded, and clapped Junior briefly on the shoulder. "I trust you to keep her safe," Cole said, as the other men began to move. Junior merely nodded, withdrew his pistol, and removed his bandanna.

"I know what Pearson's capable of," Junior said.

Cole frowned, but nodded. "You do. Your time will

come, Junior." He leaned in and spoke so low, no one but Junior could hear him. "You're the only one I'd trust her to."

Junior stood taller, his chest expanding with pride. He nodded. "Yes, sir," was all he said, but Cole knew Junior would take his charge seriously.

And without another word, he left Junior as sentry, marching to the head of the pack of men in the hall. They moved as one in stealthy silence.

• • • • • • •

The first part of their plan—the hijack—had been in effect for months, though the initial plans hadn't involved Monty and his men. The train would be arriving any minute, carrying goods that would be easily found and taken. If everything had fallen into place, no harm would come to the train conductor. The theft would be smooth, the casualties with this raid nonexistent. A simple heist and on they'd go to their final destination. Simple robberies were rare for Cole, but when Pearson had mentioned the possibility months prior, Cole saw his chance to prove himself every bit the outlaw. He needed Pearson, and now Monty, to know he was fearless and capable. If he couldn't prove himself, it would be difficult to bring about their ultimate demise.

Cole fell into step beside Monty as they came to the railroad tracks that lay on the outskirts of the forest, kneeling quickly to be sure the rails been sufficiently jostled loose, as instructed. Sure enough, the heavy metal of the train tracks, just below where the pines overlapped tall cedars, casting shadow to the ground below, were unnaturally crisscrossed, askew like violently broken bones. A train moving at high speed through the ravaged tracks would careen into the woods, but measures had been taken to slow the speed of the train before it hit the broken tracks, not for the safety of the passengers aboard, for there were to be no passengers save the driver, but rather for the safety of those who would overtake the train when it was time.

They lay in the darkness, crouched, watching the dim light indicating the ascent of the rising sun on the horizon. Cole was next to Monty, Doc on his right, Monty's men on either side of the tracks. Cole pulled out his pocket watch. The train was twenty minutes behind. Cole thought of Aida, alone with Junior as guard. The longer he left her alone, the more likely it would be that she could be harmed. Where was the goddamned train? But just as his frustration boiled, he heard the screech and whine of the train tracks in the distance. The men around him tensed, and Cole prepared for what he'd have to do next. If all went well, Pearson and Monty would be assured of his allegiance to their side. It was essential they trust him.

Down barreled the hulking form of the soot-black train, the whistle sounding in the distance, smoke billowing from atop the roof.

"Here," Cole murmured to Monty. "Just at the bend." It was where he'd given explicit instructions for the rail ties to be broken, the train tracks loosened. As if on cue, the sleek form of the train, the light illuminating the early morning darkness, veered off, and with a sickening screech of brakes and metal on metal, the train careened off its tracks and tumbled over like a bear that had been shot on its hind legs, a powerful force of nature suddenly off kilter and disturbingly erratic. It was all planned, though, and the train coming at half speed was far less violent an end than it could've been otherwise.

"Go," hissed Cole, and like snakes slithering in tall grass ready to strike, the men advanced on the train. Cole broke through the door first. The train tipped to its side, so he walked over tilted chairs and windows, and went straight to the engine room. When Cole came in, the conductor held up his hands in surrender, Cole gave a knowing nod, and the man fell in line. Cole pretended he didn't recognize Preach's jowls and dark eyes.

He gestured for him to follow in line, but the second Preach realized they were alone, he turned to Cole. "They're here," he said. Cole looked at him sharply.

Preach shook his head. "They weren't supposed to come, I know." Preach was the only one who'd been completely appraised of his initial plans, though Junior and Doc knew enough to keep them loyal. It had been planned for months, the second part of their plan only a recent development. Preach's going ahead of him had only worked to solidify their plan. They'd rob the morning train, prove to Pearson and Monty they were capable of such a hijack, no passengers to injure, and bring Pearson and Monty to justice.

"Come again?" Cole whispered.

"They're here," Preach repeated. "Wasn't a vacant train like on the record. I had to play like I knew what was happening. They had it planned from the beginning, supposedly for safety reasons. I had to go along with it, Cole, and had no way to contact you."

"Which ones are here?" Cole asked.

Preach swallowed. "The one who matters."

Cole closed his eyes. The familiar cold metal against his waist, and tucked into his boot… all it would take would be one clean shot. Preach would have him protected and be sure no one witnessed the murder. They could do anything at this point, murder him in cold blood and toss his body in the river. Shoot him and somehow feign he'd been murdered in the accident. Hell, even scalping or hanging, or some other such violent act of justice seemed fitting.

Their plans had changed, but ultimate justice would still happen. He'd find a way.

"Where's the safe?" Cole growled.

"Last car, and Monty and his men already have it," Preach said, gesturing out the window, to where Monty and three men were hauling a safe out of the last caboose. Good. At least that part of the plan had worked.

"And your passengers?" Cole asked.

Preach jerked his chin to the back. "Second to last cabin," he stated. It was hard work trotting through the rubble and debris, but Cole found them. He hoped they were injured but still alive. A sudden death for the man he was hunting would be far too easy an end.

It was all he could do to not sneer when he saw them. Whereas others would've perhaps valiantly tried to dig their way out of the rubble, or to make it to safety, the two well-dressed men in the middle caboose were huddled together like the pussies they were.

Cole knew him right away. He had the same stark blue eyes as his daughter.

CHAPTER FOURTEEN

Into the darkness they go, the wise and the lovely. — *Edna St. Vincent Millay*

The screeching of metal clashing woke Aida. At first, she reached instinctively for the warmth of the man she'd fallen asleep beside, but instead saw a tawny head in a thin stream of light that came from the darkened window. She sat up with a gasp, barely stifling a scream.

"It's just me," Junior said, holding his palms facing her in surrender. "Cole had something to tend to, and I'm here to keep you safe," he said.

She pulled the blanket up over her. Why couldn't she have gone with him? Why did he have to leave her here? She twisted in bed, her body still ached from the strapping and harsh lovemaking of the night before. It surprised her how strongly she felt the sense of longing.

"When will he be back?" she whispered, but Junior was at the window now, looking out wistfully. It was still too dark for them to see a thing.

"When he's good and ready," Junior said tersely. Aida knew Junior likely wished he was with Cole and the others, rather than playing nanny to a half-clothed woman who kept asking questions, but it still irritated her.

She threw the blanket over her shoulders and marched toward the bathroom, but Junior held up a hand and handed her a bundle of folded clothing. "Cole said you were to have this," he said. "He had someone in the saloon bring it up. A connection he has." She snatched it out of his hand and opened it up, revealing a simple gown that would fit her well.

"Thank you," she said shyly, a faint flush creeping to her cheeks as she suddenly remembered how her other dress now lay in tatters. She turned from Junior and went back toward the tiny privy, shared with a door on the other side by an adjacent room.

In a fit of anger, she threw the deadbolt on the door to keep Junior out, and flounced herself over to the sink where a small looking glass reflected her angry countenance. She looked a right mess, with her hair piled up on her head in wild ringlets, a splotch of red on one cheek from leaning up against the pillow. Tentatively, she lifted her skirt and tried to peer at her reddened backside. Had he left stripe marks?

Why was it she wished he had?

Sighing, she dressed quickly. Just as she was finishing she heard the lock fumble, and she turned to face Junior.

"You stay out of—" she began, but to her surprise, it wasn't the door she'd entered that was being jostled. She wheeled just in time to see Pearson's narrowed eyes fall on hers in victory. His thin, rabid face grew hungry, and she could only stare as he advanced.

"All alone, are we?" he asked. Just as she opened her mouth to scream, his hand reached out and silenced her, his large palm over her mouth as she pushed and struggled. He withdrew his revolver and with a sharp crack, hit her on the side of the head. She sank into darkness.

CHAPTER FIFTEEN

Hell is empty. All the devils are here. — William Shakespeare

It was an easy matter gagging and blindfolding the senators, and Cole was none too gentle when he tied the restraints on Senator Perkins' wrists. The man called out in pain, and Cole pulled harder. With them secured, his mind now raced with what to do next.

"No way to get you word," Preach said gruffly. "When we passed hands at the station, I was told a hefty sum of silver was passed across the palm of the station master." Of course the station master hadn't been aware of the planned theft that was to take place upon the train. His contact on the railroad line knew exactly when the train would pass through, exactly the amount of money held in the safe, and it had been an easy matter to bribe him into making a quick change with drivers.

Monty and his men, along with Doc and Justice, were supposed to have been in the back room with the safe, as Monty's man Rinaldo was an expert at cracking safes. Pearson would get a cut for covering their whereabouts, and several of Monty's men would take off in various directions, muddying their tracks. The state senators were supposed to be on their way toward a convention, and apparently had decided to take an earlier ride. Cole had expected them to arrive a few days later. Now what would they do with the senators?

There was muttering and cursing apparently going on behind the gags, and Cole gladly kneed the back of the man he held in his hands now. The man cried out, and Cole took a sadistic pleasure in having caused him pain. Bastard.

Cole dragged one man, and Preach the other, a thin-nosed, scrawny man with a shock of thick dark hair. Cole finally found where Monty had the safe, and he brought the two hostages in with him.

"Didn't know these bastards would be joining us," Cole said. They could be hanged for manhandling politicians.

"These men are restrained," he said. "Take them to Lawson's for questioning, and we'll have to figure out what to do with them later. I'm going to get back up and bring Junior down here." What he didn't tell them all was that his intention was to make sure he had Aida secured. She'd lose it when she found out her father was in the same building as she was and he wanted to be with her when she found out.

Climbing up the narrow staircase, he nearly ran into Junior, his eyes wide and guilty-looking as he met Cole.

"She's gone," he said.

Cold twisted in his stomach and Cole grabbed Junior by the shirt collar. "Where is she?"

"I don't know," Junior began. "She went to the bathroom and took a long time. After a while, when she didn't answer my knocks, I worried, and broke the door down. She was gone, and there was blood." Junior scrubbed a hand across his face. He looked pained. Cole itched to punch him, to throw his fist into Junior and take out his anger. How could Junior have let him down? Cole had trusted him.

"We'll comb every room in this place until we find her," Cole said. "She can't have gone far."

Where had she gone? It had to be Pearson. He'd *kill* him. Desperation made him furious, and it was all he could do not to lose his temper again. He *had* to stay in control. He hadn't gotten to where he was without staying in control.

CHAPTER SIXTEEN

I do not speak as I think, I do not think as I should, and so it all goes on in helpless darkness. — Franz Kafka

Aida trembled as she woke. Her head felt like it would split apart, and when she cracked open her eyes, the light made it throb. Just her luck, she thought. Twice now in one week to be taken against her will. But she'd do anything to be back with the *first* man who'd taken her. The wicked hands of the man who now held her made her want to vomit. He was right next to her, and to her horror, she felt him come even closer.

"He thinks you're all his," Pearson said as he pulled her to him. He ran his tongue along her collarbone. She cringed, yanking away from him, but he lifted his hand and smacked her straight across the face. Her head snapped back, pain radiating across her cheek. She screamed, but it was no use. Pearson likely thought Cole still occupied with whatever he'd gone to do, or unlikely to come fetch her.

"He's a real man now," Pearson said. "Well, real men share their women."

"When he finds out what you've done, he'll kill you," Aida hissed. He would, she knew he would. God, but she wanted him here.

Pearson grinned. "Is that right? He won't find you in time. I'll die a happy man."

He reached a hand out to her and she kicked him with all her might, straight between the knees. He howled, but only for a second before he lunged at her. She poked her fingers out, sinking her fingers into his eyeballs. He screamed in fury and pain as she found her target. As he doubled over, she kicked him again, as hard as she could. She didn't even take time to see if he was following her. She ran.

Where could she go? The long halls were filled with doors and several staircases, but she ran as far from the sounds of the man in pursuit behind her as she could. She felt him grab her skirts, but she shook him off and ran on and felt a thrill of victory as he tripped. She paused just long enough to hear him cry out in pain and see him fall to the floor. She used the distraction to her full advantage and ran faster. It sounded as if she'd lost him. Now she could hear voices ahead of her. Were those ahead of her trustworthy? Would they keep her safe or hand her over? There was only one she could trust and he was nowhere to be found.

Standing up against the wall, she held her breath. She pushed open the door and froze. In front of her was not the man she'd hoped, or even men who would help her, but the lewd grimaces of the men who'd come to camp with them—Monty and his crew. And in front of Monty was a man tied to a chair, whose profile she'd recognize anywhere—her father! How had her father come to be not only here, but held hostage like this? She turned to go but it was no use. The men standing around him had seen her, and were already advancing on her. She'd run straight from the frying pan into the fire.

CHAPTER SEVENTEEN

I loved her, but the dark side of her... her demons are what drove me wild, her secrets, her pain, her darkness... that's what made me love her. — Michael Marquez

Cole raced down the hallways, throwing open doors and searching frantically, unable to call out to Aida lest he draw attention to himself. If the authorities came before he was able to do what he had to, all would be lost. They wouldn't know why he'd done what he had, and he'd be taken, jailed, or hanged. But what was worse, Aida would be unprotected.

"For God's sake, split up," he hissed at Junior. A faint sound echoed in the hall. Was his mind playing tricks on him, or was that what he thought it was? It echoed again, and this time there was no mistaking the familiar sound of a woman's scream, a scream he knew all too well from having drawn it from the woman himself.

"It's her," he hissed to Junior. "Quick. We need to see where she is." They followed the sounds of her screams until they suddenly stopped, muffled.

Cole ran as fast as he could. Everything was a jumble. Nothing was going right. Where was she? Where was Pearson? And where was Preach? It would all work out. It had to. He hadn't come this far for everything to go to hell. The narrow staircases and dusty hallways were like a hideous maze designed to keep him away from her.

A loud *bang* echoed in the hallway. His heart stopped. Good God, had Aida been shot? He had to find her. He had to protect her. One last scream sounded, and this time it was right nearby, behind a door at the end of the staircase. He leapt off the last two stairs and kicked the door open.

In front of him stood Monty, his gun pointed straight at Cole's chest, holding onto Aida in one arm, in front of the senator. The second politician already lay slumped over in his chair, bound. God, what had Monty done?

"Well, look who's arrived," Monty said. "If it isn't my accomplice. The man who kidnapped the girl and meant for her to be ransom, eh? This isn't how we planned things, Cole," Monty said, as he drew a slow, wicked smile. "Not at all. You think you were one step ahead. Your hostage, you said. And look how you come running for her when she's *my* prisoner." His smile vanished. "Who runs after a hostage?"

"Let my daughter go!" screamed the senator. His gag had been removed now but he was still bound. Without batting an eyelash, Monty pulled the trigger, and the senator howled in pain, blood spurting from the top of his boot. Beside Cole, Junior jumped.

"Make one move and I'll kill you," Monty said to the senator. Cole knew that he would. He'd slipped out of the hands of the authorities so many times, and he'd do it again. It was why Cole had agreed to his job to begin with. Pearson and Monty were unstoppable. The senator was panting now, his eyes closed shut, but it was Aida who spoke next.

"I'd rather be killed than go back to you," Aida hissed, hatred in her eyes.

"I could make that happen, sweetheart," Monty said, pointing his revolver at Aida's temple.

"Hush, Aida," Cole ordered. Damn it all, if there was ever a time she had to obey him, it was now.

"You! You were the one who stole her from me!" the senator screamed at Cole.

Monty looked from Aida to Cole and his grin was wicked. "And you fell for her," Monty said. "Tried to make it look like you didn't. Pearson fell for it. I never did. And now you'll give her to me, and your share of the spoils today, or I'll give you up. I know who you really are." He paused as he cocked his gun. "And you should really be careful what you tell your brother."

The door burst open and Pearson stood, brandishing his gun. Monty sobered as Pearson took it all in.

"All of you go to hell," Pearson growled.

Something had to be done, and it had to be done now. Cole met Junior's eyes across the room. Cole gave a barely perceptible nod. Junior's foot shot out, kicking over a chair that stood next to him, and with the distraction, Junior tackled Pearson.

Pearson's gun went off with a deafening bang, but Cole was already on the floor, rolling, dodging the shots that Monty aimed at him as he cocked his own pistol and shot. Down went Monty, Aida falling with him. Cole howled as piercing pain jabbed him in the foot. Pearson had somehow managed to escape Junior's tackle and now was at him with a dagger. Cole smacked his gun at the back of Pearson's head at the same time Junior shot.

Monty rose on his elbow just as Cole grabbed Aida, threw her to the floor, and threw his body over her. One aim, three men he wanted dead, but it was clear Junior was not going down without a fight. Another shot rang, and Pearson slumped to the floor in a heap. Monty lunged at Cole, knocking the senator's chair to the floor as he tried to tear Cole off Aida, but it was no use. Someone would shoot him dead before he'd allow her to be harmed. Monty shot at Cole and missed, as Junior came to Cole's side, his aim sure and steady. A second shot hit Monty square between the eyes and Aida shrieked beneath him as Monty slumped on top of the two of them.

"Cole!" shouted Junior. "The senator!"

Cole snapped his eyes to the senator, who had somehow managed to free his hands with his fall and now held a gun to them both. Without a second thought, Cole pulled the trigger. It seemed to happen in slow motion. The gun dropped from the senator's hand. His head rolled to the side. The clatter of the gun on the floor echoed in the narrow room as crimson blood stained the senator's shirt. Junior stood staring at Cole, panting, and it took a minute for Cole to feel comfortable allowing Aida up from beneath him.

"You're safe now, darlin'," he whispered to her as she shuddered, and he glanced over at the now dead forms of Pearson, Monty, and the senator. "Now you're safe with me."

CHAPTER EIGHTEEN

This thing of darkness I acknowledge mine. — *William Shakespeare*

She couldn't stop trembling. How was she supposed to stop it? Her hands shook as if someone was violently shaking her about the shoulders. Her father lay dead on the floor, the other filthy men piled in with them. Cole was shouting orders to the other men she was now familiar with, but she only noticed Doc and Preach. Immediately after he'd shouted instructions, Doc and Preach were hauling bodies out of the room, Junior standing guard lest anyone come running. But however they managed it, they knew what they were doing. Where was Justice? Where had they all gone to? It was all too much, too confusing, and she couldn't understand how it was all happening, or why.

And who was Cole?

"He's dead," she whispered. "Cole, he's dead," but he didn't reply, merely kept her tucked under his arm as he moved with decision and purpose.

"Justice and Monty's men have moved the safe to Litchfield already," Cole said to Junior. "They left before anything happened and won't be the wiser for it. You go now, take the fastest horse we have, and you don't stop until you meet—" he paused and glanced at Aida before continuing, "—our connection in Litchfield. She'll know what to do."

She?

Aida tried to speak but couldn't. She opened her mouth. No words would come. As Junior raced ahead of Cole, he pulled her into the doorway of a room, and it took her a few minutes to realize it was the room they'd spent the night in. He closed the door shut tight behind them, sat on the bed, and drew her onto his lap.

"C'mere, darlin'," he said softly. She sat on his knee, buried her head on his chest, but no tears would come. He stilled her trembling hands with his work-worn hands.

"You had to think I was one of them."

She shook her head. Still, no words would come.

"You'll see in Litchfield, Aida. You'll see everything."

"He's dead," she whispered. "He's dead."

"They all are," he whispered back. "But you're safe." He pulled her head to his mouth fiercely, kissing her so that his whiskers brushed her forehead. "Put your head on Daddy, darlin'," he said. "No one's gonna hurt you now. You're mine, little one. I came for you and I made you obey me, but I knew you were mine."

"Daddy," she whispered, closing her eyes.

***

Later, she remembered the hooded cloak he put about her as they moved in the stillness to retrieve their horses, and how his own bandanna and hat cast him into shadow. She remembered how he gave her commands, to keep her head down, to follow him, to talk to no one, and how easy it was to do what he said for she had only one instruction: obey. Preach and Doc followed behind, as Junior had gone on ahead.

They galloped in the early morning light, dust rising in

billows from beneath the pounding hooves of his horse. He held her close, his body pushed up against her. His flank was to her back, his arms around her, holding her as if he never wanted to let her go.

CHAPTER NINETEEN

I will love you through the darkness. — Christopher Poindexter

Litchfield loomed in front of them now, after a long day's hard riding.

They'd stopped for a brief meal and still, Aida hadn't spoken. Cole had handed her food, hardtack, and coffee and she'd stared at him as if she had no idea what to do.

"Eat, little girl," he'd ordered quietly but she'd merely blinked at him.

"Aida," he'd warned. For a moment, he'd considered spanking her, not harshly, but enough to shake her out of her stupor. But she'd been hurt by all that had transpired, and he thought a different approach would now help.

"This happens to people who've witnessed trauma," Doc said to him. "Give her time, Cole. Be gentle. She'll come around."

So instead, he took her upon his knee, his back to the other men, and fed her himself, speaking in low, hushed tones though they were rushed. She obeyed him, eating from his hand, and when it was time to go, he hoisted her upon his saddle. He felt as if he were taking care of a small child as her little hand slipped into his. It was a feeling he quite enjoyed.

Now, as dark began to descend once again, they came to the entrance to Litchfield.

"It's important you obey me, Aida," he warned. "You *must* obey me."

"Yes, Daddy," she said simply.

Though he liked her compliance, he now wished for a bit of her spirit to return. He wanted to know she was all right. But he had other, more pressing matters to attend to.

"Straight to the stable," Cole said. "They'll meet us there."

When they pulled up to the stable, Cole felt apprehension growing. What would happen, now that the plans were so askew? Had Junior arrived ahead of them? Had he gotten word to those who needed it most? In the darkness, two shadows emerged. He recognized Junior's slight form, and the sweeping skirts of a tall woman who held herself erect until the riders came into view. She ran straight at Preach. Preach pulled to a stop and fairly leapt off his horse, taking the woman into his arms and kissing her. But it was Aida's reaction he was most focused on.

He felt her sit up and her grip on his shirt tighten. She gasped. Slowly, he guided his horse to a stop and prepared to let her down, but she was already slipping from the saddle.

"Aida, you wait," he ordered, but she didn't, was already down and running toward the woman who stood with Preach. Cole came up behind her as quickly as he could. They had to be quiet, had to be discreet, as the last plans fell into place. A part of him surged with hope and joy as he looked at her face, though he feared being heard. Her eyes were bright with tears as she held onto the woman who embraced her back.

Cole tipped his hat at the woman as he came to Aida's side.

"Lucille," he said. "We need to get to cover."

Aida turned to Cole, her eyes wide. "You know Lucille?"

she asked.

Cole grinned. "You could say that, darlin'. Now let's get you inside."

"Inside where?" she asked. "I just found her! And you want me to leave already?"

He clenched his jaw. Damn it, the girl needed to mind him. "To safety, Aida. *Now.*"

Lucille nodded, giving Aida a gentle shove toward Cole. "There will be time to catch up," she said. "But we need to make sure you're all safe."

Preach's arm went around Lucille as Doc led their horses to the stable. Aida frowned but followed Cole to where he ushered her. He eyed her. He could almost feel her willful resistance. She seemed angry, and on the verge of tears. Christ, if crying wasn't exactly what the girl needed.

There would be time, but he knew how he would bring her to where she needed to be.

***

Aida sat at a table in the back of a darkened room in Litchfield.

"I sent them, honey," Lucille said gently, taking Aida's hand in her own. The woman she'd known since she was a baby, the only one she'd ever known as mother, now sat with her, explaining why everything had transpired. She gestured to Preach and Cole. Junior and Doc had retired to their rooms, and Aida now sat with a cup of hot tea next to Cole. He'd removed his hat and watched her now with weary eyes, as the truth unfolded.

"My brother is sheriff here in Litchfield, and the only honest law-abiding man I know. Preach knew that Monty and Pearson and their men were unstoppable, and he also knew he and Mr. Clemens were the only ones Monty and Pearson trusted."

"It was the only way we could bring them out," Preach said. "Stage a high-end robbery." His eyes flitted to Cole.

"And Justice has been in bed with them for the past year."

"Where are they all now?" Aida asked. It was all so much to take in.

"You know Monty and Pearson were killed," Cole said.

Aida flinched. They weren't the only ones who'd been killed.

"Lucille was waiting here for her brother, knew that Justice and the rest of Monty's men would be running to Litchfield with their prize. They walked right into the trap set, and were all caught."

Aida gasped. "Will they hang?"

Cole looked away and worked his jaw for a moment before speaking. "Yes." He ran a hand over his face and she knew then how hard this had all been, how hard it would be yet.

She breathed out, before she resumed speaking. "And what will come of you two? Are you still running from the law?"

Lucille shook her head. "They were commissioned, honey. They *are* the law."

Aida's eyes widened. "You two?"

Cole nodded.

Lucille continued. "My brother knew the only way to bring Monty and Pearson to justice would be if one of their own betrayed them. Cole has been working for months to gain their trust so that they could be brought to justice."

Cole flinched at the word *justice* and Aida's heart went out to him.

"And Justice was part of their group?"

Cole nodded soberly.

Aida frowned. "But... what about me? How do I fit into all of this?"

"That's where I come in," Lucille said. "I didn't leave you because I needed to leave, Aida. I left because I knew you needed to be free from the home you were in, and had no means to do so. *I* sent them to get you. It was on their way, and I knew I could trust them to bring you here."

But Aida was still trying to understand. She turned to Cole. "You told me he owed you money. He didn't?"

Cole shook his head. She could forgive the lie. She'd been rescued. Her tormentor was dead.

Aida turned to Lucille. "You knew he was… treating me the way he did?" she asked quietly.

Lucille nodded. "He was an awful man," she whispered. "You weren't the only one he mistreated. I'm not sorry to hear of his demise."

"Nor am I," Aida whispered. She turned to Cole. "Did you know?"

He shook his head. "All I was told was that you had to get out of there, and I knew I trusted the source. Wasn't until you told me that I knew why."

"There was no way to get you out of there in daylight," Lucille said. "And Cole and his men had to continue to pretend to be outlaws. Kidnapping you solidified our plan. It rousted your father, convinced Monty they were on the same side, got you out of there."

Aida frowned. It seemed a more sympathetic plan now, but Cole… he'd spanked her. He'd taken her. He'd forced her to eat with them… but had he ever really violated her? No. She'd wanted his dominance and control, and though he'd always been stern with her, he'd ultimately had her best interests in mind.

My gripe is not with you…

Over and over he'd told her to listen to him, that it would all make sense in the end. She looked from Lucille to Cole. Cole was looking at her curiously, as if she were unpredictable and he was ready to handle whatever happened.

"Wasn't easy," Cole said with a bit of a smirk as he took the last swig from his frothy pint. "She put up quite a fuss."

Lucille smiled softly. "I told you she was a handful and to be prepared to deal with her."

"Oh, I was."

Aida frowned. "Yes, he was."

Lucille raised an eyebrow to Cole. "Were you rough with her, Cole?"

Cole sobered and fixed Lucille with a stern look. "What do *you* think? I told you I'd bring her here safe, but I told you I'd do it my way."

Lucille sighed.

Aida frowned. She had much to think on. So much. And she wanted to change the subject. "I'm fine, Lucille. He *was*... rough with me." She paused. How could she explain that she'd fallen for him? That he'd stripped her of her highbrow ways, and made her mind him, and shown her that the fierce, powerful side of her could roam free? That obedience to his authority freed her mind and bound her to him?

"What now?" Aida whispered.

"Whatever you want, honey," Lucille whispered back.

Aida turned to Cole and lifted her chin. Her father was gone. She had Lucille back. And the only man she'd ever trusted had turned out to be her savior. "For now, I want some sleep," she said. "And I'll stay with Cole."

Lucille's eyes warmed at that. "I understand," she said, squeezing Preach's hand.

Cole stood. His eyes heated as he pulled her to standing and tossed some bills on the table. "Time to get some rest, darlin'," he said.

As Preach and Lucille went ahead of them, she leaned in and whispered in his ear, "Yes, Daddy."

CHAPTER TWENTY

I love you as certain dark things are to be loved in secret, between the shadow and the soul. — Pablo Neruda

"Come here, Aida." Cole sat on the bed. She stood in front of the looking glass, adjusting her hair, taking each pin out and laying it on the dresser. When he instructed her, she did not move to obey.

"Just a minute," she said. He'd wondered how she'd react after she met Lucille and knew what his mission had been from the very beginning. He'd meant to take her forcefully, and he hadn't cared at the time if she hated him. His plan was to make her obey, and bring her safely to Lucille.

He'd never meant to fall in love with her.

"Not just a minute. You obey me," he said. "Now *come here*."

When she turned to face him, he could read her defiance, but he knew it was masking something else, something deeper. He'd probe to get to it.

"And if I don't?" she said with a lift of her chin.

He clenched his jaw. "Nothing has changed between us, Aida. You disobeyed me several times tonight. You're resisting me even though you know you're happier when you don't, and I don't just mean because I'll spank you."

Her eyes softened, and she looked away from him. She swallowed.

"Now I'll tell you one more time, before I come to fetch you. And honey? You don't want me to fetch you." He paused before speaking. "Come here, Aida. *Now*."

He watched her intake of breath, the way color rose on her cheeks and her eyes widened. He was an observant man. He well knew that though she resisted his command, it was what she craved, what she yearned for, what she needed.

She swallowed. "And if I run, what will you do when you catch me?" she asked from beneath lowered lids. Her words were black velvet, suggestive. His cock hardened.

"I'll spank you," he said firmly. "Hold you over my knee and whip you with my belt. Spank you long and hard until you beg me for forgiveness."

Her breath hitched and one slight hand went to her throat. She swallowed again and spoke in a whisper. "And if I do come to you?"

He began to roll up his shirtsleeves. The little girl was going to be soundly disciplined whether he had to chase her or she came to him willingly. "If you come to me, I will lay you across my knee and spank you. Because Daddy knows his good little girl's inside there, and my discipline will help her come back out to play." Both sleeves now rolled up, he folded his hands in his lap. "So what's it gonna be, darlin'?"

She took a deep breath and came to him. When she stood in front of him, he pulled her between his knees, brought her close, and crushed her mouth with his, briefly but fiercely. Pulling back, he spun her around and began to undress her.

"You didn't give me an option out of a spanking," she said.

"That's because there is none, darlin'. You need this."

She did not reply.

Her dress fell off her shoulders, followed by her shift.

One by one, he stripped her of each of her garments until she stood in front of him, naked and trembling. He turned her to face him.

"You've learned a lot here tonight, Aida."

"I've learned a lot since I've left my home," she responded.

He nodded as he chucked a finger under her chin. "And I have more to teach you. Over time, I want you to learn how precious you are. How strong, tenacious, and beautiful you are. It will take time but you will learn. Will you trust me to teach, darlin'?"

Her eyes filled, and she nodded wordlessly.

"You disobeyed me downstairs. You've talked back and delayed obeying me." He released her chin and stroked her hair with a large hand. "A good spanking should help you remember to obey me. And maybe forget about what troubles you for a little while."

She nodded.

"Over my lap, honey."

Slowly, she draped herself across his lap, straight across his knees. Sweet Jesus, she was so beautiful, strewn across his lap like this. So lovely.

He ran a hand down her soft, curvy backside as he spoke. "I'm spanking you tonight because you need to mind your Daddy. And because you'll feel better when you let go." Without another word, he raised his hand and brought it down with a resounding *smack*.

She gasped and the breath hissed out of her, but she stayed over his lap as his hand connected with the sharp snap of skin on skin. Over and over he spanked her with hard, punishing swats, until she began to twist and turn, little moans escaping.

"Ow, Daddy!" she protested, squirming on his leg. "I can't take any more!"

"You can and will," he said with determination, as he let loose another barrage of sharp swats. Her need to obey him was only a small part of why he spanked her. She would learn, and it would take time, but they both needed it. "You'll learn to obey me, Aida. You are mine, and I value what is mine." Another hard swat descended, followed by another. "Do you understand me?"

"Yes, Daddy," she said. Her voice was thick now, and he knew he was getting through to her. He paused the spanking and ran his hand along her reddened skin. One finger glided along her slit. She moaned and shifted. He took his hand back and spanked her again, hard.

"Are you going to obey me, Aida?"

"Yes, Daddy," she panted over his knee.

"That's my girl," he said. "My very good girl. Come here, darlin'."

He lifted her up and she buried her face on his chest.

"Shh," he said. She began to cry, quietly at first, tears leaking out of her eyes and onto his shirt, then harder, sniffling and shaking with tears. Ah. That was what she needed. He needed her to cry, and he'd gotten her to that point of release, where she could cleanse herself from what troubled her.

His cock ached to fill her, his mouth to claim her, as he lifted her, still tearstained and shuddering, onto the bed. He crawled to the end and pulled her on his chest. He needed to take her, but he needed her happy first, secure in his arms, no longer troubled or hardened but softened and content. He held her against his chest while she wept, running a hand through her golden curls and down her bare back, all the way down to her backside. She was warm to the touch but barely marked. He soothed the sting with his hand. She moaned and began to grind against his leg. Cole chuckled.

"Needy, little girl?" he asked in a guttural growl. "Does my girl need her daddy?"

"Ohhh, yes," she moaned.

Pride filled him as he lifted her and gently put her on her back. He unbuttoned his shirt, taking in her naked form, allowing his eyes to rove over the fullness of her breasts, the soft curves of her hips as he removed his shirt and tossed it to the side. He watched her eyes take in the breadth of his chest and his hardened muscles. Her hand went between her legs and she stroked, unabashedly meeting his eyes.

"Naughty little girl," he said. "You leave that for Daddy."

He knelt at the foot of the bed and drew her over to him.

"Open your legs, darlin'," he said. She grinned wickedly and obeyed. Hungrily he stroked his tongue between her folds. Her back lifted off the bed as she moved in time to his mouth.

"Oh, dear God," she moaned.

He grinned around her as he lapped at her, swirling his tongue around her sensitive nub. She was primed for him, so ready. He slid a finger into her as his tongue continued the torturous assault. He sucked then slowly ran his tongue along her sensitive parts, pumping his finger into her at the same time.

"Ohhhh," she moaned, grinding against his mouth. He'd bring her to ecstasy as many times as she needed. She'd earned this. She'd been brought through hell. She'd obeyed him. Now it was time to reward her.

She writhed beneath him, her hips jerking.

"Cole," she moaned. "Oh, God. I love you," she said, her chest rising as she came.

He lifted his mouth for one quick moment. "Take what's yours, darlin'," he said. "I love you." His mouth went back to her as her head fell to the side and she writhed, moaning in ecstasy. When she was finished, he made quick work of removing his pants, lifting her up on the bed, and flipping her onto her belly.

"Open for Daddy," he whispered in her ear.

Closing her eyes tightly, she obeyed, her chest flat on the bed as he drove into her from behind. She was warm and tight and ready. He wanted to mark her as his, submit her to him, and he reveled in her gasps of delight with every thrust of his hips. He was mounting, and she was ready to meet him. They both groaned their release at the same time, their lovemaking ending in a crescendo of tangled limbs, moans, and heat.

He finally tumbled onto the bed and pulled her onto his chest. She sighed.

"I feel so light," she whispered. "So free."

"Good girl," he said. "My very good girl. That's what I wanted from the beginning. You'll rest now. You'll rest now, knowing you're mine. You belong to me."

"Yours," she said, and as her eyes closed, he watched the relaxed contours of her face. She was home now, and so was he.

THE END

STORMY NIGHT PUBLICATIONS WOULD LIKE TO THANK YOU FOR YOUR INTEREST IN OUR BOOKS.

If you liked this book (or even if you didn't), we would really appreciate you leaving a review on the site where you purchased it. Reviews provide useful feedback for us and for our authors, and this feedback (both positive comments and constructive criticism) allows us to work even harder to make sure we provide the content our customers want to read.

If you would like to check out more books from Stormy Night Publications, if you want to learn more about our company, or if you would like to join our mailing list, please visit our website at:

www.stormynightpublications.com

Manufactured by Amazon.ca
Bolton, ON